Nat lifted me in his arms and carried me into the bedroom. It was an exotic feeling, being carried to bed, like something out of a movie. His lips didn't leave mine and my tongue explored the inside of his mouth as he lowered me to the surface of the bed and stretched out beside me.

I began to come alive with desire. My breasts ached. The nipples had grown stiff and were tugging outward as if they wished to leave my body. I wanted to attack him, to tear off his clothing. I wanted myself naked to his eyes and to his touch.

But I was afraid of scaring him off. It would be better, I thought, if I let him set the pace. So we kissed and he stroked my hair. I pressed my thighs against the bed to assuage the tingling heat that Nat had aroused between them.

"Sharon," he whispered. It wasn't a question, only a sounding of the name like a musical note. But I answered.

Sharon

A True History by Herself

A DELL/EMERALD BOOK

Published by
Emerald Books
8 / 10 West 36th Street
New York, New York 10018

Dell ® TM 681510, Dell Publishing Co., Inc.

ISBN: 0-440-08085-1

Printed in the United States of America

First printing—February 1983

Chapter 1

I had never been anywhere, really, before I left home to come to New York. If my mother had had her way, I think I'd probably still be back in Minnesota. It was my father who talked her into letting me go. I was twenty then, grown-up and ready to take on the world. I felt older then than I do now.

My father took me to the bus. My mother couldn't face it. We'd left her dissolved in tears at the kitchen table. By the time we pulled up under the big red and white Trailways sign, I was feeling a little shaky myself. Not shaken in my resolve to go. But the moment we got out of the car and my father lifted up the hatchback and hauled out my two suitcases, I started trembling and I couldn't stop.

He bought my ticket—his voice sounded a little gruffer than usual when he said the words "one way"— and then we walked over to the gate where the New

York bus was loading. Neither of us said much. He gave my bags to the driver, who tossed them into the dark luggage bay beneath the bus.

Then, while the bus driver waited, tapping his ticket punch with discreet impatience, my father wrapped his big bear arms around me and hugged me. I think his eyes were glistening a little when he pulled back. I couldn't tell for sure. Mine were overflowing.

"Just meet the ball, honey," he told me. "Don't try to power it. Just hit it where it's pitched."

I wasn't coming to New York to be a ballplayer. That was just the way my father talked. Some of you may remember him—Eddie "Two Leaf" Clover, a major league infielder in the fifties. My father was what is called a journeyman ballplayer. He played eight seasons in the major leagues for a total of eleven different teams. In one year alone—1956, I think it was—he played for the Pirates, the Cards and the Dodgers. He had a good glove and a weak bat. His career average was .236. He was considered a smart ballplayer. You'd have to be smart to last eight years in the major leagues with a career average of .236. He could have gone into coaching when he retired, or even have become a manager. But he met my mother while he was playing for the Milwaukee Braves, and that was that. She didn't want him traveling around seven months out of the year. So he opened a sporting goods store in Minneapolis.

He used to coach the neighborhood kids in the summer. It was very impressive, you can imagine, for these kids to learn at the hands of somebody who had played alongside Eddie Matthews and Hank Aaron, who had faced the fearsome fast ball of Sandy Koufax (albeit without much success). I was the regular short-stop. You might think it was just because he was my father that I got to play, but in fact until I was thirteen I was probably the best shortstop for my age in the county.

Then my chest started to develop. In one startling winter I went from flat-chested tomboy to Raquel Welch. It wasn't so obvious during the long Minnesota winter, while the cold weather kept me in sweaters and parkas. But when the snows melted and the smell of newly mown hay scented the air with spring again and the sound of hickory smacking horsehide began to crackle through the weekend mornings, I could no longer keep the secret I had guarded from October through March. When I took the field that April day, I was not the shortstop who had hung up her glove the previous fall.

I tried to ignore it and just play ball, but it was no good. My tits got in the way. Both literally and figuratively. The guys treated me differently. They didn't tag the same. They wouldn't slide hard into second to break up the double play. Pitchers would sulk if I got a base hit or (God forbid) a long ball off of them.

My father never actually said anything to me. But I know he was relieved when I quit. I tried to make a joke of it. "Look at it this way, Daddy," I said, "you're not losing a shortstop, you're gaining a daughter." He laughed and kissed me. I'd hoped he'd at least put up an argument, but he didn't. I went up to the room over the garage that was my private hide-out and I cried. Shortstops don't cry but girls do, I told myself bitterly, as I indulged myself in one of the fringe benefits of my sudden metamorphosis.

But after a little while crying lost its novelty, and I

3

began casting about for something else to do with the rest of my life. It must have something to do with suffering, that much was clear. For a while I thought I might be a folk singer, like Joan Baez. I made my father buy me a guitar to fill the place in my life vacated by my fielder's mitt. I spent hours above the garage fingering chords and keening Elizabethan love songs. Often my friend Mandy Greeley would come over and we would work out harmonies.

I idolized Mandy. She was everything I wanted to be. For one thing, she was practically sixteen. For another, she looked like Joan Baez. She had long black hair that hung straight down her back, where mine was red and curly. She had a thin, sensitive face with high cheekbones and big, intense brown eyes with sweeping lashes. At thirteen my face was round with nary a hint of cheekbone and my redhead's eyelashes were practically invisible.

And Mandy was as flat as a pancake.

That I envied her more than anything. With a build like hers I might still be playing short and batting leadoff. Well, that wasn't so important anymore. I had put my athletic career behind me with surprising ease. But I hated the great balloons that had blossomed over my rib cage and made me conspicuous all of a sudden.

Mandy was pleased with her figure. She was going to be a dancer. "A dancer has to be streamlined," she told me. Once up in the garage room we took off our tops and compared. Her torso was sleek, with small attractive swells tipped with tiny dark nipples. Mine loomed out, large unwelcome strangers in the familiar landscape of my body.

"They're kind of neat," Mandy allowed, looking

4

at my tits in the mirror as we stood side by side. "If you're not going to be a dancer, I mean."

"I hate them," I said unhappily.

"Let's see how they compare from the side view."

We turned facing each other, glancing over our shoulders at our mirrored reflection. It was even worse. Mandy's body seemed all of a piece, while mine was an assemblage of two different people. We stood so that our breasts touched, and it seemed to me that she was standing closer to me than I was to her.

Then I became aware that my nipples were hardening and pressing against hers. I didn't know what that meant, but it embarrassed me. I turned away and put on my shirt.

At the start of my senior year in high school, my parents gave me a typewriter. I took it to my garage room, set it up on my desk, and sat down at it. It was an Olivetti portable, black with white letters and chrome trim. It smelled of newness and machine oil. No smell had hit me with such a visceral impact since my prepubescent years when the fragrances of spring meant baseball to me. I ran my fingers over the keys, feeling a shudder of excitement ripple through my body. In that moment a writer was born.

For the rest of that year I wrote, and I read. I wrote seventeen short stories and I devoured the writings of Jane Austen, the Brontës, Thomas Wolfe, Joyce Carol Oates, D.H. Lawrence, F. Scott Fitzgerald and Edith Wharton. The following fall I entered the University of Minnesota. I threw away all the short stories I had written, began a novel, and began reading James Joyce, Thomas Pynchon and Franz Kafka. In my sophomore year I scrapped the novel, tried a play, read the classic Russian authors, and subscribed to half a dozen small literary magazines.

By the end of my sophomore year I concluded that I could progress no further where I was. I needed a change of environment if I ever was going to develop as a writer. I needed to leave home, school and Minnesota, and take a crack at the real world.

I had to get to New York.

Chapter 2

I asked the cab to wait while I rang the bell. The name was written like an artist's signature in oil paint on a scrap of paper in a little metal slot. Toliver. There was no response. I pushed the button again.

The cabbie was getting restless. He had been scribbling on his trip chart. Now he stuck it along with the pencil into a rubber band on the sun visor.

"What do you want I should do, lady?" He was Greek or Lithuanian or something. The name on the license had been long and indecipherable and his speech was thick and difficult to understand.

"Couldn't you wait another minute?"

"Not unless I turn on the meter again."

"Oh, no. . . ."

I meant it as dismay, but he took it as dismissal. With a shrug and a cloud of carbon monoxide he was gone. I was alone on a deserted street in a strange, warehousey section of New York called SoHo, at eleven o'clock at night. I felt tears and perspiration spring simultaneously from my body's water supply. A door opened across the street and a man stepped onto the sidewalk. He started across toward me. I was ready to scream, but he veered off toward the corner and disappeared from view. I leaned on the buzzer again.

"Yes?"

"Mr. Toliver?" I cried into the intercom.

"Yeah, who is it?"

"It's Sharon Clover! Mandy Greeley's friend!"

"Oh. Okay, I'll be right down."

He buzzed me in and I waited by the elevator door. My knees were shaking with relief. I couldn't imagine what I would have done if he hadn't been there. I hadn't called because Mandy didn't give me his telephone number.

"It's Zebulon Toliver, on Spring Street," she had told me. "There can't be too many of those."

No, but it turned out there was something in New York called an unlisted number. And Zebulon Toliver had one.

The elevator cables whirred and clanked behind industrial grey doors. "It's a loft building," Mandy had warned me. "It used to be a toilet seat factory. Don't expect one of those slick Manhattan high-rises you see on television." And indeed this was anything but slick. The cheap electronic modernism of the intercom was the closest thing to style that the building had to offer from the outside. The small foyer was covered with grey paint that had been indifferently applied a long time ago. I stood flanked by my two suitcases and my typewriter, waiting for a fifty-year-old elevator to arrive with somebody named Zebulon Toliver who was supposed to give me Mandy's keys. Zebulon Toliver. I was prepared for a Gabby Hayes, with patched overalls and a tobacco-stained beard.

The elevator door rattled open. A young man stood inside. He was tall and slim, with dark hair that hung down near his shoulders. His eyes were a hazel color, sleepy lidded. His jaw was lean, with a ridge of definition that ran from his cheekbones around his mouth to a deeply cleft chin. He wore a denim shirt that was flecked with a confetti of oil colors and threadbare faded jeans held by a turquoise-buckled belt that was the only clue to where his hips would be.

He held out his hand. "Hi, I'm Zeb Toliver."

"Pleased to meet you." I was so flustered I practically curtsied. I had never seen anyone that good-looking in person. I wondered why Mandy hadn't said anything to me about him.

He took my suitcases and moved them onto the elevator, and I followed them in. "Here are your keys." He held out a small ring and identified them to me. "The silver one's the street door . . . this one's the back door, off the stairs . . . and this one gets you off the elevator."

"You need a key to get off the elevator?"

"Sure. It opens right onto the loft. You don't want people just dropping in, do you?"

I thought that I wouldn't mind Zeb Toliver just dropping in. After a rocky start, my New York adventure was beginning to go much better. I'd already made up my mind that Zeb Toliver was going to be my first New York affair.

"What do you do?" I asked as the elevator groaned and started its climb.

"I'm a painter."

"Oh really? That's great! I'm a writer."

"Are you?" He smiled. "Good for you."

We reached the fourth floor and the door slid open. "Here you are," he announced, swinging my bags out. "Make yourself at home. I'm two floors up, on the top floor. Just give a holler if you need anything."

"I will," I promised. But the door had already closed.

I was to have Mandy's apartment to myself for the next three months. She was touring with her dance company in Europe and Australia. She had given me her place to stay in, rent-free, until she got back in September. I was sorry not to have Mandy around to introduce me to her New York world. But it would be wonderful to have a home that would provide both solitude for writing and relief from the financial pressures of paying rent. By the time Mandy returned I hoped to have gotten established with a publisher.

Mandy's apartment was beautiful. I had expected a garret, but the loft was huge. It occupied the whole floor of the building, with polished wood floors, high ceilings and huge leaded windows. The walls were exposed brick and there was a labyrinth of pipes crisscrossing the ceiling. There were no separate rooms as such, except the bathroom. Instead, the different spaces were defined simply by the arrangement of the furniture and plants. The bedroom was a suspended platform reached by a beautiful curving wooden staircase.

Lush greenery sprang everywhere from pots, planters and window boxes. Large unframed canvases lined the walls with a variety of styles—abstract, photo realist, neoimpressionist. Near the area of the suspended bedroom one caught my eye. It was a nude, sprawled against bright pillows in a sensuous pose. One hand was poised lightly on her dark pubic mound; the other propped up a head that gazed with mocking challenge at the viewer. It was Mandy.

Perhaps it shocked me a little. But it was a positive shock. I felt like a young Colette arriving in Paris, the provincial girl landing in the middle of the bubbling artistic cauldron, ready to add her pinch of genius to complete the recipe.

I stood for some minutes caught in Mandy's erotic gaze. Then I moved closer and looked at the signature in the lower right corner of the canvas. I recognized the signature even before I read the name itself. It was identical to the one I had seen in the metal slot downstairs.

Toliver.

My mind raced ahead. He would paint me, of course. An arresting nude that would catch me in this moment of my life: sophisticated, yet still bedewed with innocence; the talent that would soon become famous already visible in those smoldering eyes, the girl-woman, talent and body ripening together, budding, ready for flowering.

Or deflowering.

That was my guilty secret. I had brought a certain accursed membrane intact with me to New York. This wasn't through any philosophical devotion to virginity. Far from it. I had been ready for at least three years to take the plunge. I'd even been willing to surrender my

11

cherry to one of the loutish boys I dated back in Minnesota, just to get that monkey off my back.

The trouble was, nobody had ever made a serious assault on it. The problem certainly wasn't my looks. I had what could fairly be described as the best body at the University of Minnesota and a damned pretty face to go with it, if you didn't mind lots of frizzy red hair. No, my problem was not my looks. They were, as one of my keen-witted boyfriends once remarked to me, the stuff that wet dreams were made of.

My problem was my brain. I was smart. I read books. I wrote. I had opinions. That was the chastity belt that protected my virtue. And I couldn't slough it off. I was certainly willing, in my frustration, to fuck a fool; but I couldn't bring myself to give the boy the satisfaction of thinking *he* was fucking a fool.

It was probably my virginity as much as my literary ambition that finally caused me to break away from my Midwestern cocoon and come to New York. The two frustrations really were rooted in the same thing. And now I was going to solve them both with one move. In New York I would be among people who would stimulate me creatively and provide me with an atmosphere in which I could grow as an artist. I would be among people for whom a beautiful woman's intellect would act as an aphrodisiac, not a threat.

I hummed as I unpacked my bags and set up my typewriter on the desk by a window. A new era was waiting in the wings. And Zeb Toliver was going to bring it on.

Chapter 3

New York that spring was an enchanted place. I would go out each morning and be seized with the feeling that the air itself was charged with a special kind of molecule in which the neutrons were double-activated. How could anyone ever be unhappy in New York? It was too alive, there was too much energy, too much to do. And I tried to do it all.

I began with the museums. I went to the Modern, the Met, the Whitney, the Guggenheim, the Frick, the Museum of the City of New York. At each one I spent days, and I knew I was only skimming the surface. I went to galleries in SoHo, in the Village, on Fifty-seventh Street, on Madison Avenue. I discovered half-price tickets at a booth on Williams Street and started going to the theater, Broadway and off-Broadway, several times a week. I went to movies, concerts, jazz clubs, rock clubs, after-hours clubs, ballet, even the Planetarium.

I prowled for hours in wonderful little bookstores. I wandered with awe through the magnificent New York Public Library on Forty-second Street, marveling at its immensity, its beauty and the vastness of its collection, and listening to the small sound of my footsteps on its marble floors.

All of this took up a great deal of time and I was forced to make certain sacrifices. For one thing, I wasn't doing any writing. But that, I told myself, could wait. Writing, I argued to the nagging voice of my conscience, was more than simply sitting down at the typewriter and banging on the keys. Writing came out of life and experience. And I was absorbing those things. When I was ready to write, I would know it.

The experience I was most anxious to undergo, however, continued to elude me. It was nearly three weeks before I managed to run into Zeb Toliver again. I had neglected to get his unlisted telephone number, and despite his invitation I was shy about going up and pounding on his door. I did muster up the courage once, but he wasn't there.

Then one day, as I was fumbling for my keys and juggling a bag of groceries at the front door, he turned up.

"Hi," he said. "Hey, let me give you a hand with that."

"Thanks."

"How's it going? Getting used to life in the big city?"

"Oh yes, thank you. I love it."

"How's the writing?"

"Um, I'm . . . I'm working on a novel."

"What's it about?"

"It's, um. . . ." I had to be careful here, I could get myself in trouble. "It's kind of autobiographical."

He gave me a dazzling smile. "Sounds like a very attractive subject."

"Oh, it is," I chirped, and then blushed as I realized what I'd said.

The elevator door opened on my floor. "Excuse me," I said, "I think I'll just get out here and kill myself."

Zeb laughed. "Don't do that. I'd never get to know you."

With an opening like that, even Sharon Clover couldn't miss. I invited him in for a drink.

"I haven't seen you," I said.

"I've been in Cleveland the past week or so, hanging a show."

I brought him a bloody mary. "I love your work."

He looked pleased. "What have you seen?"

"The one at the Whitney, the street scene. I really loved it. The way you use color and light to suggest emotion. And this one of Mandy." To my horror, I blushed. Of course he noticed.

"Does it embarrass you?"

"Oh no! No, I think it's fabulous. Don't mind me, I'm an easy blush." I shrugged hopelessly. "What can I say, I'm a real redhead."

Zeb grinned. "I'll bet you are."

I felt my face flush to a neon red. "I'm sorry," I apologized. "I'm not usually this stupid."

"You're not stupid at all. You're very charming. And very pretty. I'd like to paint you."

"You would?"

"Very much. Would you consider posing? I'd pay you, of course."

"I'd love to. When?"

"How about Thursday?"

Zeb's loft, two floors higher than mine, was much brighter. Sunlight streamed in over the rooftop of the building across the street that blocked my windows for all but two hours every day.

The model's stand was in a corner, so that light fell on it from two windows. Canvases were stacked along the walls. The kitchen and living room were at the other end of the loft and the bed was in a far corner near the fire escape. It was a queen-sized bed, made up with an eiderdown comforter. I looked at it with more than passing interest. It all went according to plan, that was where my virginity would meet its Waterloo.

Zeb was squeezing paints onto a clean piece of plywood. "There's a robe on a hook on the bathroom door," he called out. "You can undress in there."

I had dressed simply, not being sure how these things were done. I had on a denim shift, with nothing underneath. In the bathroom I slipped it off. The shower wall was all mirror and I took a last look at my virginal body. It was gorgeous. My breasts, the bane of my puberty, now looked as though they belonged. I had grown into them. They leaned out, round and inviting, with a fullness that didn't yield to any sagging. My skin was smooth and white (except for a little redhead's freckling on the shoulders) as it ran down over a tight, flat belly to the shock of bright orange fleece that covered my pubic mound. I turned and looked over my shoulder to inspect my ass. It was firm, two round

16

scoops each punctuated with a dimple at the top. My legs were long, graceful, symmetrical. Mine was a good body, I told myself, built for love. Zeb would not be disappointed. The only major flaw in it couldn't be seen . . . and by the end of this day, with any luck, it wouldn't be there.

I pinched my nipples experimentally, as a person might check the batteries in a flashlight, to make sure they were working properly. They responded beautifully. I took down the robe, wrapped it around me, and went out.

"Ready? Good. Let's see how we want you. . . ."

Zeb positioned me on a bank of cushions, lying on my stomach with my head propped up on one hand and the other crossed beneath my breasts. My legs were slightly spread apart, with one knee bent. He touched me several times as he lined up the pose, each time sending chills of pleasure and anticipation through me. I was sure he could feel it too.

He painted for about two hours, giving me a couple of breaks to stretch. We talked very little. It was an extraordinary feeling, living there in the apartment of the man to whom I had mentally promised my maidenhead, stark naked, while his eyes constantly scrutinized every inch of my body. The soft exposed fleece between my parted thighs grew damp with anticipation. . . .

Suddenly he threw aside his paintbrush with a strangled moan. In two steps he was at my side, taking me in his arms. He covered my face with kisses. "Oh God, Sharon," he murmured passionately into my hair, "forgive me, but I couldn't stand it anymore!"

17

I stroked his head. "It's all right, my darling, it's all right."

His lips moved feverishly down across my alabaster skin, exciting every place they touched. They burned at my throat, my shoulder, the upper swells of my breasts. When at last he fastened them upon a nipple, I cried aloud. I crushed him to me, feeling the mad flickering of his rough tongue drive cascades of sensation through the rigid tissue, and spread uncontrollably throughout my body.

He lowered me upon the multicolored group of pillows. My heart was knocking against my ribs, my breath was coming in short ragged gasps. Impatiently he tore off his shirt and flung it aside. I had a moment to admire the rippling washboard musculature of his stomach before his hands went to the turquoise buckle at his waist and pushed down his jeans.

I gasped in spite of myself when his cock sprang free. Purple-headed and thick, it was a good foot long. I had fantasized about a cock this big, but seeing it now, looming over me, it suddenly filled me with terror.

"Please," I said in a small, quavering voice, "I'm a virgin."

Zeb knelt beside me. "Don't worry," he said gently. "I won't hurt you. We'll go as slow as you like. We won't do anything you don't want to."

His voice reassured me. Gratefully, curiously, I reached out a hand and touched the stiff blind giant that protruded from his groin. It was hot to the touch and vibrated as if from a powerful motor humming somewhere deep down inside it. Zeb sat patiently, not moving. I rubbed my thumb across the engorged head and it bucked as a spasm went through it. A small drop

*of moisture collected at the pinprick opening at the end.
I leaned forward and licked it away.*

*I began to run my tongue around the swollen tip of
his cock. My fear had been replaced by fascination,
and something else: a craving to have this huge beast
inside me. I touched it lightly with the fingertips of both
hands, gauging its size. It was awesome. I opened my
mouth wide and slid my lips over it. The head alone
totally filled my mouth. I massaged it with my tongue
and tried to suck it deeper, succeeding in cramming a
couple more inches in before it mashed against the back
of my throat and I had to give it up.*

*With a quick movement, Zeb pivoted his body,
swinging his knee across to straddle my shoulders and
burying his face in the wet red down of my virginal
pussy. His tongue began to explore with deft long strokes
that ran from my clitoris down to the tight cleft of my
buttocks. I raised my hips to meet him. At the same time
I caught hold with both hands onto his cock, which was
now extending down to me like some monstrous stalac-
tite, and brought it to my mouth again.*

*His tongue began to shorten its sweep, concentrat-
ing on the hard button of sensation at the top of my
cunt. Excitement built in me and I gobbled insanely at
the massive spear of flesh in my mouth as my first
orgasm erupted and broke over me like lava. My thighs
flew up and locked around the back of Zeb's neck. I
squeezed his face hard against the wet pulse that seemed
to be my entire being.*

*And then he moved around so that his legs were
between my legs, his cock touching the lips of my
pussy.*

"Will it . . . ?"

"It might hurt a little. Tell me you don't want it, and I won't."

"Don't want it? Oh, Zeb!" I arched my back, spreading my thighs wide and seizing him in my hands to guide him into me. My lips parted and he slid inside until the thin wall of my cherry stopped him.

He looked into my eyes. I hesitated for just a moment, not from any lingering fear or doubt, but to capture the moment forever. Then I nodded. He pushed forward, and broke through, and filled me. . . .

That was how it should have happened. That was how I wrote it later, but the scene was fiction. Pure romantic projection, the outpourings of a frustrated virgin's imagination. Which probably accounts for the somewhat overblown style of the prose.

What did happen was precisely nothing. At about four-thirty Zeb Toliver stepped back, squinted at the canvas and said, "Well, that's it for today. You can get dressed now."

Dressed?

"Don't you want to . . . do any more?" I asked.

"No, not today. Light's starting to go. I'll do some work on it over the weekend. How about another session Monday?"

I went back into the bathroom, crestfallen. The body I saw in the mirror was the same one that had been there before, inside and out. The alchemy I had expected hadn't taken place.

This business of falling from purity was going to be trickier than I had thought. Even in New York.

Chapter 4

The Lion's Head is a bar on Sheridan Square in Greenwich Village that has a reputation of being a hangout for writers. As soon as I heard about this, I made a beeline for the place.

I got there at ten o'clock on a Friday night. The entrance was down a couple of stairs from the street. When I walked through the door a few heads turned to look at me, but I headed in as if I was meeting someone. The place was packed. I was reasonably confident that if they weren't all famous writers, at least there were famous writers among them. The trouble was, I had no idea which ones.

I found a tiny opening at the bar and squeezed in. As I waited for the bartender to get to me, I contemplated the important decision of what I would order. What do writers drink? I looked down the bar, conducting a silent, informal poll. There was a lot of beer in evidence, but I've never liked beer. I would drink it if necessary, but perhaps there was an alternative.

At the end of the bar, a man with a florid round face topped with snowy white hair was drinking some kind of whiskey from a shot glass, washing it down with beer. Next to him was a man in a tweed jacket and tie who had a short glass that looked like it contained Scotch on the rocks. There was a woman with them. She had a loose, sloppy figure and a pretty face, with grey-streaked hair tied back in a bun. She was drinking something that looked like white wine, but I couldn't be sure. As I watched, the bartender came over to them and the white-haired man winked and made a circular motion with a downward-pointing finger.

"Another round? Right you are, Mr. Flaherty," said the bartender. I watched like a hawk. Watney's ale went into the beer glass, some kind of Irish whiskey into the shot glass. The tweed jacket got Johnnie Walker Red. And for the lady, he poured from a bottle of Pernod.

Pernod! That was something a writer could drink. Prepared now, I tried to catch the bartender's eye.

As I waited, the stool next to me was filled by a young man wearing a dark blue pinstriped suit and a blue striped shirt with a high white collar and a necktie. His sandy hair was cut close at the neck and was parted in the middle. His face, which I could see only in profile, was handsome, with a strong nose, square jaw and eyes of a deep sky blue. The expression mingled arrogance and poetry. He looked like a character out of *The Great Gatsby*.

The bartender came our way.

"What'll it be, folks?"

"Pernod, please."

"I'll have a martini cocktail," said my neighbor. That was how he said it. *A martini cocktail.*

He looked at me and smiled. "Seems as though he thinks we're together."

"Yes," I agreed, "it looks that way."

"No reason to embarrass him." He held out his hand. "I'm Liam McCorley."

"Hi. I'm Sharon Clover."

We got our drinks.

"I haven't seen you in here before," he said.

"No," I replied. "I've . . . I've been away."

"Oh? Where?"

I wasn't about to admit that I had just arrived from a lifetime in Minnesota. "Paris," I lied smoothly.

"Paris," he nodded. "Great town. How long were you there?"

"Oh, a year. . . ."

He seemed impressed. "Where'd you live?"

"Do you know Paris?" I stalled for time, racking my brain for details of the Truffaut pictures I had seen in college.

"Not too well," he admitted.

"I had a little place on the Left Bank. Rue Madeleine." Well, it was a Cagney movie, not Truffaut. But I was pretty sure it was Paris.

"What were you doing there? Studying?"

"Writing."

"You're a writer?"

"Sure, why not?" I was a bit defensive.

"What sort of thing? Journalism?"

"No, I'm working on a novel."

"Ever been published?"

23

It was too risky. "No," I admitted.

"Well." He smiled encouragingly. "It takes time."

From this I understood that he had been published. In spite of myself, I was impressed. But I thought it was too soon to let on. I didn't want Liam McCorley thinking I was a hick.

"And what do you do?" I asked him.

"I'm a drunkard." He said this with a slight mocking curve of his lips. To emphasize the point, he drained his martini and signaled to the bartender. "Another one, Harry." He looked at me. "Another?"

"Sure."

"A citizen of barrooms international," he amplified. "And a fugitive from justice."

"No! You're a fugitive from justice?"

"From the justice of the written word. On the lam from my own typewriter."

"A lapsed writer?"

He smiled at me appreciatively. "Not only beautiful, but with a gift for the right phrase." He removed the olive from his second martini, sucked it with a little popping noise of his lips, and then dropped it back into the gin.

"So you've taken refuge in drink?" I prodded him.

"Everyone suspects himself of at least one of the cardinal virtues, and this is mine: I am one of the few truly degenerate people I have ever known."

"Talk about gift for phrasing," I laughed. But somehow the line had a naggingly familiar sound to it. I tried for a brief moment to place it, then shrugged it off. "I probably should know this, but I'll take a chance and ask. What have you written?"

"You mean, what have I published?"

"That, yes."

He stared broodingly into the shallow pool of his martini. "*Home In That Rock*."

I shook my head apologetically. "I'm afraid I don't know it."

"No? It was in *TriQuarterly*."

"Oh."

"Never heard of it, have you?"

"What, *TriQuarterly*? Sure."

"It was also included in the Pushcart Prize that year."

"That's terrific!"

"Nominated by John Gardner."

At last we were moving to familiar ground. "Oh, he's great," I said. "Well—I'm very impressed." Subsequent research did nothing to lessen that impressiveness. *TriQuarterly*, it developed, was a highly respected literary magazine published at Northwestern and the Pushcart Prize was a critically acclaimed anthology of the best of the small presses, put out every year by the Pushcart Press. I even went to the library and found the edition of Pushcart Prize that Liam's story had appeared in. It was very good, if a bit derivative of Thomas Wolfe in style.

But this was several weeks later. I'm still talking about the night I met Liam, and that night was far from over.

After a while we left the Lion's Head together and walked east. We stopped in a couple more bars—"gin mills," he called them—and by the time we reached his place on Bleecker Street he was pretty well gone. I was feeling the effects myself after a half-dozen glasses of Pernod.

"This," he said solemnly, with a sweeping gesture that took in a studiously nondescript brick building near the corner of MacDougal Street, "is where I live. May I invite you up for a nightcap?"

"I would be nonplused," I answered, feeling somehow that it was the wrong word, but unable to zero in on anything more appropriate.

He started up the steps to the front door, lost his balance, and walked backwards with passable dignity to the sidewalk again. "So we beat on," he declaimed, "boats against the current, borne back ceaselessly into the past."

This I recognized, even from deep beneath six fathoms of Pernod. "Fitzgerald," I said.

"Yes?"

"I mean . . . oh, never mind. I'm not sure what I mean."

"What you need is a drink."

Liam lived in a studio apartment on the fourth floor. The bed, a Castro convertible, was unfolded and unmade. On the walls were a couple of Riviera travel posters and an unframed John Held, Jr. reproduction of a dancing flapper that had been cut from a magazine. The bar was a collection of bottles atop the chest of drawers.

"Gin?"

"No, Pernod."

"No Pernod."

"No?"

"No."

26

I settled for white wine. Liam poured himself half a glass of straight gin.

"Why don't we sit here?" he said, indicating the bed. There was virtually nowhere else in the room to sit.

"All right." I was feeling reckless. Would he try to seduce me? It seemed a virtual certainty. And why not? It wasn't the dashing defloration I had pictured for myself with Zeb Toliver, but it had the advantage of being a bird in the hand. Liam was very handsome. And he was a published writer.

And perhaps it would be better in the long run not to come to Zeb Toliver a virgin. Virginity scared some men. With that telltale membrane gone, I could easily pass for a woman of experience. There would be no way of telling that I was a veteran of only a single encounter.

My cherry wasn't likely to put much of a scare into Liam McCorley. In his condition, I would be very surprised if he even noticed it.

He began nuzzling my neck. I put my drink on the night table. His hands fumbled with the buttons on my blouse. I waited patiently, caressing his hair. It took him a while, but he got the buttons undone.

"Mmm," I sighed.

He pushed my blouse off my shoulders. "Good God," he said, "what's this?"

I took it at first to be a compliment to my tits. Then I realized he was looking at my brassiere.

"It's a bra," I replied. "Haven't you ever seen one before?"

"Not in a long time."

So girls in New York didn't wear bras. I should

have realized. But out in Minnesota concepts like that took longer to filter through. It was an embarrassing mistake, but on the other hand Liam probably wouldn't remember anything about it in the morning. And by that time the bra would be long gone in the garbage.

I unhooked it myself—no sense putting his drink-thickened fingers to that unaccustomed task—and tossed it away. Liam's hands locked greedily on my full breasts. Even drunk, he had a good touch, and I began to feel the passion building up inside me. He rolled my nipples between thumb and forefinger, pulling on them until they were stiff and aching with pleasure. He began to kiss them, moving his hands away to stroke my sides, running his thumbs up into the sensitive skin of my armpits. I lay back on the bed and closed my eyes, moaning, abandoning myself to his touch.

As the momentum built his hands seemed to acquire sureness. He undid my belt without a misstep and followed quickly with the button and zipper of my jeans. I raised my hips and he pulled the jeans away, taking the panties at the same time. I felt the vacant air against my crotch. A moment later his warm breath stirred the hair between my legs. His tongue touched the wet lips of my cunt.

The effect sent a shiver of ecstasy through my whole body. We had entered a realm that was totally new to me; had entered it moments ago, really, when Liam guided my panties over my thighs, a route they had previously taken only under my own hand. My cunt had been touched before, but only by groping boys in automobiles or on the porch outside my parents' home— quick furtive squeezes, often through the fabric of my panties. One boy, Rodney Rotweiler, used to slide his hand inside my pants over my bare ass when we were making out, down past the cleft between my cheeks to wiggle a finger in the sopping wetness below. Then, as I quivered with arousal and ground my loins against him whimpering for relief, I would feel a spasm run through him and hear his sharp exhaled grunt in my ear.

But this was something new. I had fantasized being eaten, but the fact far outstripped the fantasy. Nothing my young girl's brain had been able to imagine had provided an apt simile for the feeling of the peculiar texture of tongue flesh against labia minora. Saliva-smooth, firm and flexible, it was intimate beyond belief.

"More," I moaned, "more!"

But there was to be no more. The movements of Liam's tongue had stopped. I felt a strange, rumbling (and not unpleasant) vibration. At first I thought he was unleashing some new and exotic cunnilingual technique, and I sighed and spread my thighs wider still. Then I felt it again and recognized the sound that accompanied it: a snore.

Liam McCorley had passed out.

Chapter 5

I ran into Liam again a couple of weeks later quite by accident. I was with a group of people at the Spring Street Bar when he came in. There were two girls with him. Both were brunettes. One was tall and thin, very pretty, with dark eyes and a wide angular mouth that featured a lot of white teeth when she smiled. The other was rounder, short, given a bit to overweight, but sensual. They took a table near the back.

He hadn't seen me. It was just as well; I was not inclined to speak to him. There are few insults more difficult for a woman to forgive than a man falling asleep while eating her pussy, no matter what the quantity of drink he has imbibed. Still, snubbing him would be more satisfying if he knew I was there. If he even remembered me. Which, I had to admit, wasn't very likely.

I kept glancing at him sidelong. Once I thought I

caught his eye, although in the dim bustle of the room I couldn't be sure. I turned coldly away, refocusing my attention on my group. I was with two painters, an actor who doubled as a cab driver, a woman who I think was some sort of social worker, a poet and a sculptress. The actor was trying to put the make on me. He was about forty, past his days as a leading man, trying painfully to make the transition to character actor. He had just auditioned that afternoon for a life insurance commercial. He talked as if he didn't care whether he got it or not—it was just a "gag," he said—but I got the feeling that it was of desperate importance to him. And that he had very little chance of getting it.

He was describing the agency casting system to me when I felt a tap on my shoulder. I looked up and saw Liam standing over me.

"It is you, isn't it," he said. "I thought so."

"I think you must be mistaken," I insisted.

"No, don't you remember? We met at the Lion's Head a few weeks ago. Your name is . . . wait, don't tell me."

"Don't worry, I won't."

"Sharon, right? Sharon Glover."

"Clover. I'm afraid I don't remember. . . ."

Liam laughed. "To tell you the truth, I don't remember much about that evening myself. I believe I got a little tight. But I remember meeting you. The important things stick with me."

It was hard to keep cold-shouldering him if he really had no recollection of his mortal insult to me. I decided to test him further. "I do remember talking to somebody one night. Were you there the night we all went on to the Bitter End?"

32

Sharon

"Could be. All I remember is meeting you, talking. You'd just come back from Paris, right? And from there on my mind is a blank. I woke up the next morning in my apartment with a rotten headache."

So I wound up deciding to forgive him. It seemed very much a case of a tree falling in the forest and nobody being there to hear it. Philosophically speaking, it had never happened. I was inclined to be philosophical.

Liam and his two friends joined us. The plump one's name was Marielle Garmitsch. She did something with fabric design. The tall one was Gabby Lazare. She was a writer who Liam had known in college. She was apparently living with a lawyer and working on a novel. She also wrote articles for various art publications.

"Liam says you lived in Paris. Is that what your book's about?"

"Some of it."

"How's it coming?"

"Oh. . . ."

"Yeah, I know the feeling. Sometimes I just get stopped cold. The group helps. Are you in a group?"

"No . . . I don't think so. What kind of a group?"

"A writer's group."

I never heard of a writer's group. She explained.

"We get together twice a month and read aloud from works in progress. Then we throw it open for discussion and criticism. It gives you some feedback."

I said, "I don't think I could do that. A bunch of strangers sitting there tearing me apart would make me nervous."

Gabby laughed, showing those strong white teeth. "It's not like that," she told me. "Well, not usually.

33

Sometimes you do need a thick skin, but mostly the talk is pretty helpful. Oh, and it's all women.''

''I don't know if I like the sound of that.''

''Believe me, it's better. You concentrate on the writing, not on sexual maneuvering. And there's no macho heavy-handedness.''

''Well, yes, I see what you mean.''

''Come some time,'' she invited. ''I'll call you next time we get together. Just come and sit in, see how it strikes you.''

''I'll think about it,'' I said.

When I got back to the loft there was a message for me on Mandy's answering machine from a Dr. Pavelich's secretary. She said it concerned my father and left a number to call.

My heart hammered as the phone rang. After the fifth ring a man's voice answered. ''Dr. Pavelich speaking.''

''Dr. Pavelich, this is Sharon Clover. Is my father all right?''

''Sure he is. At least, he was this afternoon. He asked me to call you and see how you were doing.''

I sighed with relief. ''I guess I haven't been too good about writing. Are you an old friend of Daddy's?''

''I sure am. Well, now that I've got you, how are you doing?''

''Oh, fine, thank you.''

''Meeting people? Making friends? Getting enough to eat?''

''Yes, sir, I am.''

''Good! I'd certainly like to have a look at you for myself, just to see what Eddie Clover's little girl looks like, so I can make a firsthand report to your dad. Suppose you let me take you out to dinner to-night.''

''Well, I. . . .''

''Unless you have other plans.''

Liam had asked me to meet him at the Lion's Head later. I had told him I didn't think I could make it. But I knew that as the evening wore on, I'd probably break down and go over there. Now I wouldn't have to. And a meal out in a good restaurant sounded appealing.

''No, nothing important,'' I said. ''I'd love to.''

I bathed, did my hair, and put on a dress I hadn't had out of the closet since I arrived in New York. It was a purple gauze, soft and loose, worn low on the shoulders. It was trimmed with white lace at the sleeves and along the hemline and I wore it with a gold belt. It was a little sexier than the occasion called for, but it was the only glamorous thing I had. I really wanted Dr. Pavelich to make a good report to the folks back home.

It felt good to be dressed up. I completed the effect with some blusher, eyeshadow and a little lipstick, and dabbed Shalimar behind each ear and in my cleavage. I called a taxi, not wanting to wander around the neighborhood looking like this. Somebody might recognize me.

We were dining at Clos Normand. It was a lovely restaurant, with quiet colors and roughhewn wooden beams that gave it the look of a French country inn—or what I imagined a French country inn ought to look like. The walls were painted with murals of Normandy.

I made a good entrance. Heads turned and I could tell they liked what they saw. I told the maitre d' that I was meeting Dr. Pavelich. He led me through the crowded, noisy dining room to a table where a balding, heavy man of about sixty was sitting.

Dr. Pavelich rose to greet me. "Sharon?" he asked. "Well, my goodness!" He took me by the shoulders and kissed me warmly on the cheek. "I've never met your mother, but she must be a lovely woman. You certainly didn't get your looks from Eddie."

Dinner was wonderful. We began with an appetizer of mussels steamed in their own juices with shallots, herbs, milk and wine. I ordered the quenelles with lobster sauce, Dr. Pavelich had the duckling, and the waiter suggested a French white wine that was very good. As we ate, Dr. Pavelich told me how he and my father had become friends.

"I was the team physician for the Brooklyn Dodgers when your father played here. I saw a lot of Eddie. He was a tough, scrappy ballplayer, one of the fiercest competitors I ever saw. The sight of old 'Two Leaf' Clover barreling into second base with his spikes high shook the nerve out of more than one shortstop trying to turn the double play. And strong! That bat he used—a forty-inch Louisville slugger, had to be darned near as big as he was. He could whip that thing around like it was a fly swatter." Dr. Pavelich shook his head appreciatively. "Yes, sir, Eddie Clover. He could have been one of the great ones in my opinion, if he hadn't banged himself up so much. That's how he got his nickname. Your dad just didn't seem to play in much luck. His first season up with the Cards, he'd worked his way into the starting line-up by the middle of June and he was hitting something like .340, when he tripped over the rolled-up tarp chasing a foul ball back of first base and cracked his head against the railing. The next

year it was something else, and something else again
after that. That's how I came to spend so much time
with him. He was always coming up with strains and
chips and fractures. Nothing kept him down for long,
though. I was always very fond of your dad. We've
kept in touch.''

"Are you still in a sports practice?''

"Oh, yes, I see a lot of athletes. Runners, a lot of
runners. Tennis players. I still see a few ballplayers,
though I'm not associated with a team anymore.''

Dr. Pavelich had a genial, horsy face, with an
exceptionally long jaw and wide, leather-colored lips.
All that remained of his hair was a fringe of white that
hooked over his ears in fluffy sideburns and scalloped
down in back to hem the base of his skull. He had
broad shoulders and looked as if he might once have
been an athlete himself, but his paunch now dominated
his physique.

"So, how is your writing coming, Sharon?'' he
asked me as the waiter brought our coffee.

"I'm really working away at it, Dr. Pavelich,'' I
assured him, sipping my espresso. It was strong and
good. Unlike my work habits, I thought, picturing the
dusty typewriter standing neglected on the desk at home.

"You writers,'' he said admiringly. "Don't see
how you do it. I don't see how you come up with ideas.
Where do you get 'em from?''

"They just . . . come to you. You've just got to
sit there at the typewriter and sweat it out sometimes.''

"Isn't that something! What's your book about,
honey?''

"It's sort of autobiographical. It's about growing
up.''

"Hey, hey, I bet Eddie's going to love reading that. Every parent wonders what goes on in his kids' minds when they're growing up. How many hours a day do you put in?"

"I try to do at least five or six."

"That's a long time to sit at a typewriter."

"I know. Sometimes my back gets so sore. . . ."

"Does it? Where?" He reached across the table and touched the bare skin of my back about three inches below the nape of the neck. "Right about in there?"

"Yes!" I agreed. It seemed the logical place for my back to hurt if I really had been typing six hours a day.

"It could be structural," he advised me. "Sometimes a minor adjustment is all it takes to straighten out a thing like that." Dr. Pavelich took out his American Express card and laid it on the check. The waiter, who had been hovering unobtrusively, swooped down, pounced on it and carried it away.

"Why don't you step around to my office after dinner," Dr. Pavelich suggested. "I'll have a look at it."

"Oh no, that's okay. It's really not that bad."

"Nonsense. It's just around the corner, no trouble at all. I told Eddie I'd make sure you were all right—I can hardly just leave you with an aching back now, can I?"

I protested in vain. For a moment I panicked that he would check out my back and be able to tell that there was no tightness, deduce that I had not been writing at all, and report back to my parents. On the other hand, maybe he could straighten something out. I had in fact suffered some backaches in college when I'd been doing a lot of typing. And I was going to be starting to work again very soon. Preventive medicine was the best kind, they said.

Dr. Pavelich's office was one of those ground floor offices whose dull green bronze shingles are a staple of Fifth Avenue ambiance. We crossed a spacious waiting room that was done all in grey, with Matisse prints on the walls. He stopped and glanced at some papers on the receptionist's desk, then led me into a white examining room off the corridor.

"Let's have a look," he said. He brought me over to stand in front of a full-length three-way mirror, the kind you find in a clothing store. "Stand naturally," he instructed.

I drew my shoulders back and pulled my tummy in the way we had been taught to "stand up straight" as children. Dr. Pavelich shook his head with a chuckle.

"Ho-ho, not like that." He shook my shoulders gently to take out the stiffness, then put one large hand on my waist and the other palm flat against my chest. "Like this," he corrected, pushing me gently.

"Oh," I was a little embarrassed—not that he had touched my breasts; he was a doctor, after all. But I was afraid he would notice that I wasn't wearing a bra.

Dr. Pavelich ran his fingertips down my spine, from the base of my neck to the crease in my buttocks. "That's your problem, right there. Alignment's all out of whack, as we say in the medical profession. No wonder you get backaches. I'm glad you came to see me. In twenty years you could be walking like an old lady if this isn't taken care of."

I was a little shaken. "What do you think I should do?"

"Get undressed."

I looked at him in surprise. "But I. . . ."

He waved a hand impatiently. "Behind that screen." He glanced quickly at his watch. I was keeping him from something, I saw. It was rude and inconsiderate of me to bring modesty into this now. He was doing me a favor. I hurried behind the screen and took off my dress and sandals. Wearing nothing but my panties, I stepped back around the screen.

His back was to me.

"Dr. Pavelich . . . I'm ready," I said.

He turned around, and I thought I heard a sharp intake of breath. Then he frowned. "I told you to undress," he said sternly.

"Yes, but . . . I thought you meant. . . ."

"Take off those—what do you call them?"

"Panties?"

"Mm, yes. Take them off too. I am trying to conduct an examination."

"I'm sorry . . . should I . . . ?" I indicated the screen, totally flustered now at my maladroit behavior, and blushing a beet red.

"No, no." He shook his head. I hooked my thumbs in the waistband of my panties and slipped them off.

"Good," said Dr. Pavelich gruffly. "Now come and stand here by the mirror again. Do you see? Do you see the curvature?"

I saw my naked body reproduced in triplicate in the mirror's panels. I saw plenty of curvature. "Yes," I said.

"Lie down there on the table."

There was an examining table in the middle of the room. I went over to it. "On my stomach?" I asked timidly.

40

"Ummm . . . yes."

I lay face down. His hands began to move along my back. His fingertips pushed against my shoulders and dug up under the shelf of the shoulder blades. He pressed hard with his thumbs against the muscle tissue at either side of my neck. He brought his fingers down my spine and ribs, exploring, probing, testing. When he reached my waist he pressed in hard with both hands.

"Do you feel that?" he asked.

"Yes." It felt like a tight corset. I realized that it was making the cheeks of my ass spread out. I fought the embarrassment. He was a doctor, I kept reminding myself. And an old friend of my father's.

"Yes." His hands moved down over the mounds of my buttocks. "Yes, you have a real . . . a real. . . ." His voice trailed away for a moment.

"I am going to try something that may have an effect. This may feel a little peculiar, but don't worry."

I could see that he had moved over to the utility table. He was putting on a thin latex glove. He squeezed something from a tube and rubbed it onto the middle finger of his right hand.

"Just relax now," he told me as he came back to where I was lying. His bare hand returned to my cheeks, spreading them apart. Then I jumped and gasped aloud as I felt his lubricated finger penetrate my asshole.

"Relax!" he commanded, in a voice that had become noticeably more gravelly, as he pressed down hard against the small of my back with his free hand. I tried to relax; but the feeling of that digit lodged deep in my anal canal sent wild sensations through me. My pussy began to pulse and grow wet. I buried my face in the examining table in shame.

"This," Dr. Pavelich explained hoarsely, "enables us to see just how the internal structure of the lower lumbar region is arranged." As he spoke his finger began to move slowly in and out. In spite of every effort to control it, I found that my hips were beginning to undulate in an involuntary motion. A little whimper escaped my lips.

"Good," he praised, "good!"

His finger was moving faster now and I could no longer make any pretense at controlling the writhing of my hips. I turned my head and saw to my astonishment that Dr. Pavelich was tugging down his pants. His cock, fully erect and rooted in a tangle of grey hair, sprang into my view for a moment.

"Now," he cried, "we restructure!"

With an agility that I couldn't have imagined when I observed his hanging paunch in the restaurant, he pivoted and leapt astride me, plunging his cock down into the soft wet nest of my pussy. For a brief moment the barrier held, and for that moment time froze for me. It set the instant apart, limned in neon, to be called up at will for review—as I do now, writing this. The fat stomach fitted against the deep curve of my back and ass, the aged erection straining against the young seal of my virginity . . . and then it broke, he tumbled in, and with a few frenetic strokes he was spent.

Dr. Pavelich was silent as I dressed, except for a few shamefaced, mumbled apologies. The red stain on the white sheet of the examining table was the mute reproach that struck at him. I think he was terrified that

Eddie "Two Leaf" Clover would come barreling out of the Midwest, spikes high and brandishing a forty-inch Louisville slugger, to avenge the betrayer of his daughter's innocence.

I said nothing to relieve his discomfort. But in fact I wasn't distressed. There could have been no one more perfectly chosen to be the agent of that transformation. My secret shame had been disposed of, by a man whose opinion meant less than nothing to me.

And of course, I need never worry now about Blue Cross.

Chapter 6

I had posed twice more for Zeb Toliver and still nothing happened. The painting was nearly finished. I decided that it was time I took matters into my own hands.

On a hot summer night in early July I went out to the liquor store and invested in a chilled bottle of Moët & Chandon. I put two of Mandy's wine glasses in the freezer. I took a cool scented bath and Shalimared myself everywhere I had reason to hope it might be noticed. I put on a beautiful Japanese kimono of Mandy's that I had found in the closet. There was nothing underneath but my fresh and fragrant body. I removed the champagne from the fridge, the glasses from the freezer, and climbed out the back window onto the fire escape.

Norm and Abby, the couple who lived in the fifth floor loft, were out. That removed any danger of detection. The buildings across the way were industrial lofts and were deserted at this hour of the night. Zeb's light glowed two floors above me. I scampered up the slatted iron steps toward its beacon.

I didn't see Zeb at first as I peered in through the window. His television set was on. A moment later Zeb came into my line of vision.

He was naked.

His body was as beautiful as I'd known it would be. Not excessively muscular, but perfectly proportioned and toned. His stomach was flat, with just a light growth of hair that stretched from the center of his chest down his middle to join the thick curls at his groin. His cock was not quite the monster I had pictured in my fantasy, but it was big enough.

He had apparently just come out of the shower and was toweling himself off. I stayed a moment in my secret observation post, drinking in his sensual beauty. Zeb put down the towel and picked up a rolled joint from the table. Then he half-turned in my direction and smiled, and for a moment I thought he'd seen me. But he couldn't have, and I decided it must have been what was on the television that had drawn his grin.

He lit the joint and dragged deeply on it. Now was the time. I took a deep breath and moved toward the window.

Then I stopped cold. Zeb held out the joint toward the large round swivel chair that sat with its back to me. A hand reached out and took it.

I felt a cold chill run down my spine. I pressed myself back against the railing. Another second, and I would have committed a dreadful faux pas. Part of me thought I should go, but the voyeur in me wanted to

46

stay and watch. Then something happened that eliminated any doubt.

Zeb took a final drag on the joint and placed it in an ashtray. Then he went to the chair and swiveled it toward him. Curled up in it, smiling an inviting smile, was a slim and gorgeous boy of about nineteen.

Zeb knelt down in front of him and took his head in his hands. He pulled the boy's face to his, pressing his lips to those smiling lips. Their mouths stayed together for a long time and I watched fascinated as the boy's slim dark cock rose out of his lap and pointed eagerly at Zeb Toliver's breastbone.

Still kissing, Zeb brought up his hand and began to stroke the boy's thigh, moving his hand in widening circles until it began to brush against the blond copse of pubic hair, finally against the jutting erection itself. I heard the boy moan. His legs unfurled and stretched out as he slid forward to offer his cock to Zeb.

Zeb sat back, resting his buttocks on his heels, and smiled sardonically at the young blond.

"Hey c'mon, man, don't be a fuckin' tease," the boy pleaded.

"What's your hurry, Perry? We've got all night. It doesn't do to rush these things." Zeb grinned softly and reached out to take the quivering shaft in a feather touch with his fingertips. With a delicacy that must have been excruciating, he moved his hand down along the rigid flesh, then up again as slowly. The boy squirmed and closed his eyes in a grimace. Beyond his shoulder Dick Cavett smirked on the television set as the studio audience chuckled its approval of his wit.

"Easy, now," Zeb crooned. He brought his other hand into play, sliding it up the channel of the boy's parted thighs to tickle at his balls. The boy spread his legs wider and slumped down so that he was virtually horizontal. The chair had twisted so that I now had a view almost directly up into his crotch. My own fingers began to stray toward my moistening cunt as I squatted in the darkness of the fire escape and watched Zeb toy with his lover.

"Please," the boy begged.

"What? What do you want?"

"I want you to suck my cock! I want you to fuck me!"

Zeb drew back with a show of anger. "If you wanted a plain dumb fuck you should have gone with a sailor," he snapped. "I'm an artist." He stood up and walked away.

The boy looked stunned. Tears came into his eyes. "Oh no, please," he sniveled. "I'll do it the way you want. I'll do anything you want, but please don't stop!"

I could see Zeb's face, as the boy could not. There was a mischievous smile on it. This was a tactic, then. He wasn't really angry.

The boy came over on his knees and wrapped his arms around Zeb's thighs. He buried his face in Zeb's ass, sobbing. "Give me another chance," he cried.

Zeb turned around. His face was stern. He put a hand under the boy's chin and raised his tear-streaked face to look up at him.

"You've been a naughty, impetuous boy."

"Yes. . . ."

"What do you think I should do about it?"

The boy thought a moment. He didn't want to give the wrong answer. He bit his lip. "Spank me?" he asked hopefully.

"Only if you're truly sorry."

"But I am!"

Zeb seemed to relent. "All right, then. Bring me that hassock. Good." He sat down, pointing at his knees. "All right, then."

Obediently, eagerly, the boy stretched himself across Zeb Toliver's lap. Again the scene might have been stage managed with the fire escape seat in mind, for his smooth round ass was aimed directly at me. I could see the tip of his cock protruding below Zeb's thighs.

For a moment Zeb's long fingers caressed the waiting cheeks. Then his hand went up and whipped down again with a resounding crack. The boy's head jerked up with a bleating cry. As Zeb raised his hand again a red imprint was already forming where it had been.

Crack! The hand slapped down again, and a third time, and a fourth. The boy was squirming in pain, his cries pitiful to hear. And then I noticed that where before I had been able to see only a glimpse of the head of his penis in the space framed by the bottom of Zeb's thighs, I could now see a full couple of inches of the shaft. And as I watched it suddenly erupted, sending long spurts of thick white semen down to cloud the bright polish of the wood floor.

My own orgasm flooded my hand with warm wetness. I was afraid they might have heard my moans through the open window, but they gave no sign of it. I stood unsteadily and crept to the fire escape stairs. Looking back, I saw that the boy was now on his knees in front of Zeb, his head bobbing up and down above Zeb's lap. But I didn't want to see any more. My body was drained, my illusions were shattered. I descended the fire escape, skittering quickly past the fifth floor landing as the light came on and Norm and Abby entered their apartment.

Back inside, I opened the Moët. The glasses had long since lost their frosting, but the wine was cool. The cork shot out with a sharp report and ricocheted off the wall, landing on my pillow. I poured the champagne into a glass, drinking it slowly. Picking up the bottle, I went to sit on the bed. I flicked on the television. Dick Cavett was just leaving the air. The end credit crawl was rolling, and I couldn't make out who his guest had been. I poured another glass of champagne and settled back against the pillow. My cunt was still warm and tingling.

So Zeb Toliver was not to be my great love. Well, no matter. I hadn't come to New York for that. I had come to be a writer.

Chapter 7

I did begin writing. But the process was painful and the progress was slow. Like physical muscles, the muscles of the creative imagination are quick to turn to flab when they aren't exercised regularly. The timing is off, the reaction time slows, dexterity turns to clumsiness, phrases and images scoot away like booted double play balls. I hadn't sat down to the typewriter with seriousness of purpose since my father bought me that ticket for New York. Now I did, and I sweated and suffered.

I went with Gabby Lazare to her feminist writer's group. I didn't take any of my works. I was nowhere near ready to expose my writing to even the most supportive of scrutiny. We met in an apartment on East Thirty-fifth Street, the home of a woman named Margo Kale. She served tea, white wine, cheese and crackers. It was a sunny, characterless apartment on a high floor in a modern building. There were seven or eight women there, including me.

Margo Kale was a small, sharp woman in her late thirties. She was thin, with no figure to speak of, but she dressed stylishly. She wore her hair up. Her face gave the impression of attractiveness, although none of the individual features backed that up. Her husband had left her three months earlier.

After we had sipped tea or wine and nibbled at the hors d'oeuvres for fifteen minutes or so, gossiping in trivialities and waiting for latecomers, the session began. Celia Weinburger read a poem about the depressing view from her window that was also meant to symbolize the feminine condition. The consensus was that the imagery was good, but that it was weak on structure. Then Margo Kale read a chapter from her novel-in-progress, *Below The Belt*. It had to do with a woman who is frustrated in her relationship with a husband who cannot satisfy her intellectually, socially, culturally or sexually. At the end of the chapter she decides to take a lover.

She looked at him as he sat snoring in front of the television set where a baseball game flickered its pointlessness. A beer can hung from his fingertips, fingertips that knew nothing of a woman's needs, but could remember the necessary motor functions for holding a tepid cylinder of aluminum in his sleep.

She left him there. She put on her coat and went out. She decided to go and see Bruce. Bruce had wanted her for a long time. She was not at all sure that Bruce was the answer, but at least he would be ardent, for the time being anyhow. At least he would be better than Tad.

Heads nodded in approval as Margo finished reading.

"It's so true," observed one of the women. "That's the way they are."

"Why do men have to be so boring?"

"Why does it have to be a man?"

It was Gabby who had spoken last. Margo and the others looked at her inquiringly.

"Why have her go see Bruce?" Gabby persisted. "What is Bruce going to have to recommend him? A big cock? Look, a big cock is all very well and good, but that's not what she needs right now. And that's not what the book needs."

"What do you mean?" Margo asked, pouring herself another glass of wine.

"What's missing from Theodora's life?" one of the others asked, picking up the thread. She was a tall, outspoken woman named Billie something with prematurely grey hair and a Scarsdale address. "Almost everything, the way I read it. She doesn't just need the kind of sex a man can give her. She needs a total relationship."

"Exactly," Gabby agreed. "That's where your book has got to go now, if it's going to make the kind of statement it ought to make."

"You mean . . . ," Margo faltered, ". . . a lesbian relationship?"

"Well, don't look so shocked, dear," Billie laughed. "It does happen. Haven't you ever made love to a woman?"

"No!"

"You ought to try it. It doesn't make you a lesbian, but it can be an awfully refreshing change of pace sometimes. All a man does is fuck you. Generally speaking he doesn't want to when you do, and he wants to when you don't. But a woman makes love to you. And when you're in a woman's arms you have the most beautiful sensation of being home."

"I have to agree, Margo," Celia Weinburger said. "At this point in your book, her husband Tad is not a man, he's *all men.* So when she goes out looking for an alternative, there's really only one place she can go."

"To Emmeline."

Margo shook her head uncertainly. "I don't know. . . ."

"Look," Gabby argued, "if she goes to Bruce, he'll be sympathetic, sure. Because he wants to get in her pants. But he won't really understand her problem. And you'll just be reinforcing the old treadmill: A woman needs a man to solve her problems. But look at what we have here in this room. Women! Women solving women's problems! Right?"

"Right!" chorused a half-dozen throats.

"I think I see what you mean," said Margo eagerly. "Of course! If she goes to Emmeline she's not making the compromise that would be set up with Bruce. Sex divorced from spirit."

"We all know women are emotionally and intellectually more sophisticated than men. Here you can make that statement in a powerful and meaningful way!"

A vision sparkled in Margo's eyes. "Theodora goes to Lincoln Center. The Mostly Mozart program is just under way. She buys a ticket and slips into a seat in the rear of Alice Tully Hall. The music fills her with its aching beauty. At intermission she wipes the tears from her eyes. She feels she is being watched. She looks up. Emmeline is in a box above her. Their eyes meet. Emmeline gives an almost imperceptible nod.

"At the end of the program Theodora walks out, mingling with the crowd. Suddenly she feels a soft hand slip into hers. It is Emmeline. 'Come,' she says. . . .

"Emmeline's limousine is waiting. They get in. The fragrant leather plushness of the interior is intoxicating to Theodora. Emmeline flicks a switch. 'The park,' she says crisply to the driver. 'Just drive.' She pushes a button and a dark curtain descends behind the driver's head."

I felt my skin beginning to tingle. I glanced around the room. All the others were sitting forward in rapt attention. Celia's thin hands were bunched together and pressed deep in her lap.

"Emmeline is wearing an elegantly simple white silk jersey dress, caught at the waist with a braided rope. An identical twist of rope encircles her forehead, holding her honeyed curls. A single large ruby set in gold hangs from a gold chain between her breasts. Her turquoise eyes widen with compassion as Theodora haltingly recounts the tale of her disappointing marriage.

"Theodora lapses into silence. A tear trembles at the corner of her eye and breaks away to slide down her cheek. Emmeline leans forward and catches it with her lips. She kisses Theodora's cheek, her eyes, her mouth. Theodora is stunned, but after a moment she starts to respond. It is this, she realizes, that she has wanted all along. She parts her lips to admit Emmeline's long probing tongue, returning the caress with her own. Her hand, with a will of its own, slips inside the silken jersey to enclose Emmeline's soft breast. It is like touching an extension of herself. Their bodies shift and they are lying on the deep upholstery of the seat. Somehow their clothing falls away. . . .

"Emmeline's long fingers slide across Theodora's mound of Venus, and with a woman's sensitive touch they pluck at the strings of her soul. Theodora's lips encircle the taut nipple of Emmeline's breast, bringing the . . . oh my God!"

I couldn't tell what it was that had broken through Margo's reverie, but suddenly she was aware of the aroused fascination of her circle of listeners and of the erotic tale of feminine love she was spinning. She broke off in terrible confusion.

"No, go on!" Celia encouraged.

"I don't know what came over me," Margo gasped, jumping up and busying herself desperately with the clearing of cups and glasses.

Billie went over to her, took the tray from her hands, and set it on the counter. "It was good," she praised. "It was very good. Come with me, I want to talk to you for a moment. In private." She took Margo's hand and led her down the hall toward the bedroom.

"What did you think?" Gabby asked me as we strolled out of the elevator and into the street.

"It was very interesting. Is it always like that?"

Gabby laughed. "Today was a bit more dramatic than usual. But you could see how the group's input moved Margo to a whole new track with her plot."

"And maybe with more than her plot."

"Yes, I'd guess that by the time Billie gets through

with her this afternoon Margo'll have some firsthand
experience to draw on for that scene. But that's all part
of it too—experience, interaction, mutual help, all part
of the creative process.''

We had reached the corner. Gabby touched my
arm. ''You busy tonight? Want to have dinner with
me?''

Perhaps another time I would have been delighted.
I did happen to be free, as usual. But in the context of
the afternoon, I shied away. ''Thanks,'' I said. ''I wish
I could. But I've got a date tonight.''

She walked me to the subway entrance. We kissed
good-bye in the manner of friends, but my afternoon's
paranoia made me self-conscious about it. On the ride
home, Theodora and Emmeline replayed their passion-
ate encounter in my mind against the roar of the subway
train, interchanging from time to time with Billie and
Margo, with Gabby and myself. I was relieved when I
got home to find another message from Liam McCorley
on Mandy's answering machine. I had been putting him
off, still with some lingering resentment over our opening night fiasco. But I called him back this time and
agreed to a date. Tonight, I thought, I would feel better
going out with a man.

Chapter 8

Liam picked me up and we went to the movies. The Waverly was playing a revival of *The Mother and The Whore*, a French film about a young man and his involvement with two women. The title described the categories in which the young man put the girls between whom he was torn. It was a very good film. As we were leaving I overheard the people in front of us talking about it. They said it was a very autobiographical film by its director, Jean Eustache. The main character, played by Jean-Pierre Leaud, was Eustache as a young man. In the years since the film was made, apparently both Eustache and the girl he described as "the mother" had committed suicide. I was sorry to hear that. Liam hadn't heard the couple talking, so I was able to repeat the information as my own later when we were having dinner at a cheap Italian restaurant.

"You knew him?" Liam was impressed. Then,

suspiciously, he added: "How come you didn't say anything before we went?"

I shrugged. I tried to make it a Gallic shrug. "I thought it might seem like name-dropping."

We talked some more about the movie. "Which one did you identify with?" he asked me.

"In light of the way things worked out, I'd be a fool not to pick the whore."

"In the movie, she doesn't get him."

"No, but she's still alive. And if she had won him, she'd be a widow."

"I'd like to get to Paris," Liam said, changing the subject. "Maybe as a journalist, for a while. Give me a chance to make some money and pick up material while I work on my novel."

This was something new. On the occasions when we had talked in the past he had been disdainful of journalism, or of anything other than "serious" writing.

There were other changes in Liam. For one thing, he was growing a mustache. He dressed differently than I had seen him dress before. Gone were the elegant suits and silk ties. Gone too was the refinement of manner he had affected on sober occasions. The new Liam was more macho. He was wearing a turtleneck and a corduroy jacket. He told me he was boxing at the YMCA.

"Boxing? Why boxing?"

"It's good discipline. Like hunger. It clears the head. It's good for a writer to get in touch with himself on a basic level like that."

"I guess so."

We drank wine with dinner and later we went back to his apartment and had more wine. His apartment looked just as I remembered it from last time, except that a copy of *The Sun Also Rises* had replaced *The Great Gatsby* on his bedside table. The vodka bottles were gone from his dresser top, replaced by cheap French red wine.

When we made love later it was very good. It was something of a landmark for me: my first non-rape. Liam was a good lover. I thought he was a bit self-conscious, aware of technique and the impression he was making rather than letting it flow naturally, but that wasn't all bad. A conscious dedication to technique was better than the inconsiderate approach that many men were reputed to take.

Liam ate me first and I felt again that surge of excitement I had felt on the abortive try that other night. Naked, I spread myself on his bed and let him arouse me with his tongue and lips. He stopped once as I was beginning to build toward an orgasm. I think he was intending to come up and enter me, but I didn't want to endure a break in the momentum at that point, so I grabbed his hair and pushed his face back into my crotch. I raised my hips, ground myself against him, and he renewed his efforts. Very soon I came.

Then I let Liam up for air. "I'll do you now," I offered.

He had a beautiful body, muscular and fit. The boxing workouts at the gym must have been good for him, at that. I hadn't seen his body naked the other time. I lay alongside him and took his cock in my mouth. It was already very hard. I ran my tongue around the head, then pushed my lips farther down. I was relying on instinct and the little I had read in erotic novels for my technique—every bit as self-conscious as

Liam, I have to admit. But it seemed to be effective. He began to groan and pump it into my mouth. When he started that I pulled back a little. I didn't want Liam to come yet, and I didn't want him coming in my mouth. I wasn't sure if I would like that. But more important, I wanted him to fuck me.

I caressed his balls gently in one hand, feeling their strange rolling softness. He strained upward with his hips, trying to reach my lips again. I teased the head with the tip of my tongue for a moment, then stopped when it began twitching spastically.

"Now," I said.

He rolled me over and came up between my legs. He fumbled at the lips of my cunt with his hand, found the opening, and thrust home. After a half-dozen hard strokes he stopped his movement, groaned in anguish, and grimaced. I thought perhaps he had hurt himself.

"Are you all right?" I whispered.

"Yes. . . ."

In a few moments he started moving again, slowly, with great control. I couldn't tell whether Liam was satisfied. Then I no longer cared, as a wonderful rushing feeling began to gather at the outskirts of my body and race toward the center. I started to babble and buck my hips, digging my fingernails into Liam's back. He picked up his pace too and we came together. He collapsed heavily on top of me, breathing hard. I wrapped my arms and legs tight around him.

I asked him later about his novel.

"Could I see it? I'd love to read it."

"No. I don't show it to anybody. Not till it's finished."

"Sometimes it can help to have some feedback. Especially from another writer."

He gave me a look that said I had overstepped my bounds in suggesting that we were both the same category of being. "It wouldn't help," he said. "I work alone."

I was insulted. I started to get dressed.

"What's the matter?" he asked. "Where are you going?"

"Home."

"I thought you were going to sleep here with me."

"I sleep alone," I said.

Chapter 9

In September Mandy returned. I had been out at the racetrack with Liam. I had backed one winner and wound up the day twenty dollars ahead. Liam lost. He wouldn't tell me how much he had lost.

"I'm giving up the track," he announced glumly as we rode the subway back into Manhattan.

"You'll win next time."

"No. Horse racing is a good and a fine thing, but it takes too much time. You get too mixed up in it and it takes too much time away from writing."

Liam had been brooding a lot lately. Sometimes he was full of charm and good humor, and then we would go out and see friends and have a great time. Other times he wouldn't want to see anyone. He would sit and read, or write longhand in pencil on a yellow legal pad. He wouldn't let me see anything he wrote, but I doubt he ever let anyone else see it either. I followed his exam-

ple and refused to show him my novel. I had begun to
make some progress on it, but I was terrified of criticism at this point. I did return a few times to Gabby
Lazare's group, just to see what sort of things other
people were doing. But I didn't want them criticizing
my novel. When they began to insist that I had to show
something, I spent an afternoon writing a chapter from
a spurious feminist novel which I read to great applause.

Mandy was on the phone when I came in, sitting
on one of her half-dozen suitcases. She waved at me
animatedly.

"Sharon!" she called out when she hung up the
phone.

"Mandy! I can't believe it!"

We embraced. "I got your letter, but you didn't
say which day. I'd have been here for sure."

"I didn't know when I'd be getting here. I was in
Bangkok two days ago. My God, it's good to be back."

"You look fabulous." It was no more than the
truth. I hadn't seen Mandy since the last time she was
in Minneapolis, about three years earlier. Since then we
had written to each other regularly. Now that I saw her
again face to face, I could tell that she had matured.
Her eyes were deeper, her facial structure more sculpt-
ed. She was a strikingly beautiful woman.

I wondered if she could see the changes in me.

"How's New York been treating you?" she asked
me, holding me at arm's length for inspection. "You're
all grown up since I saw you back home. Any little
adventures?"

I laughed. "A few."

She squeezed my arm and smiled. "All grown up,
all right. So, how do you like the place?"

"It's been fantastic. Oh, Mandy, I really couldn't have swung it without you."

"I didn't do anything. The place was here, you did me a favor by occupying it. I wasn't going to sublet to strangers." She giggled. "Especially not with *that* hanging up there." She pointed at the nude.

"Oh yes," I said. "I posed for him too."

"You did? Oh damn, I should have warned you about Zeb's peculiarity."

"Too late. I found out." I described to Mandy my adventure on the fire escape. She sank back on the sofa laughing.

"Speaking of champagne," I remembered, "I have some on ice waiting for your triumphant return." I fetched the bottle and two glasses.

"To the end of your travels," I toasted, "and the beginning of mine."

"No, Sharon, you stay here. There's plenty of room."

"Thanks. But it's time I found a home of my own. If I'm going to write, I've got to be in my own space."

"Well, whatever you want. But stay here as long as you like."

"Okay. And thanks."

I was sure it wouldn't take me any time at all to find an apartment. But I quickly found out how wrong I was. Rents were sky-high. I looked in every part of Manhattan, from Inwood Hills to the Battery. I finally settled on a miserable little walkup on Broome Street. The paint was peeling, the walls were rotten, and the stairs creaked at an alarming pitch. My apartment was

on the fourth floor. It could be reached only by someone in the peak of physical condition.

"One consolation," Mandy observed, "you can
be robbed by burglars who're in good shape. Eliminates
the junkies."

Liam was less positive. "From now on we fuck at
my place," he told me. "By the time I climb all these
stairs, I'll be too tired to get it up."

He had undergone another of those curious meta-
morphoses that I had begun to grow used to in him. He
was developing an English accent, dressing in a dandi-
fied way again, and beginning to intrude references to
Roman Catholicism into conversations. It was at this
time that I finally put two and two together and figured
out what was going on.

For the latter part of the summer he had been
immersed in reading Ernest Hemingway. But lately
Hemingway books had disappeared from the tabletops
of the apartment on Bleecker Street. For a few weeks
there had been no clear successor. And now, lately,
Evelyn Waugh had begun to appear. *Decline and Fall,
A Handful of Dust, Brideshead Revisited*; and with the
new literary invasion, Liam himself seemed to take on
the trappings and idiosyncrasies of the author of the
moment.

I discussed this with Mandy.

"I don't see the harm in it," she confessed.
"Though you could be in trouble if he starts getting
hooked on Oscar Wilde."

Now that I was paying rent, I began to feel the
sharp jaws of urgency nibbling at my heels. I had been
able to conserve my savings pretty well all summer

when I was living at Mandy's, but now three hundred and fifty dollars was bolting out of my bank account with every flipped page of the monthly calendar. I couldn't last many months without either selling my novel or finding a job. I hated the thought of getting a job. I suspected I couldn't work all day and still come home with enough energy to write. It was tough enough with nothing else to do.

By mid-December I had written about a hundred and fifty pages. I was beginning to feel lost in the welter of words. I had to show my novel to somebody. The writer's group was the obvious choice, but I didn't want to open myself up to a whole panel. One person would be overwhelming enough. Liam might be too critical, all by himself. I was a bit in awe of Liam and his dark, moody genius, his stacks of yellow pads covered with secret scribblings. Everyone said he was brilliant. Gabby, who had known him at Northwestern, told me that his reputation there was as the next bright comet of American letters. I myself had read only the one story in *Pushcart Prize,* but I'd been deeply impressed by his sure technique and rich imagery. Liam's scrutiny might be more than my fledgling writer's sensibilities could take.

I decided to show my work to Mandy. My telephone was out of order, so I put the manuscript into a paper box and walked up to Spring Street. But Mandy wasn't home. I stood in the street and thought about going to see Liam. This was tempting, but too risky. I wasn't strong enough for that yet.

It was cold and a meddlesome wind was worrying bits of trash along the sidewalk. I tucked the box under my arm and headed back toward home. I ran into Liam as I turned the last corner.

"Hello, Sharon. I was just coming to see you. You busy tonight? *Ivan the Terrible Parts 1 and 2* is playing at the Bleecker. Want to go?"

I had seen this coming two weeks ago when we had stopped into a bookstore. Liam had picked up a paperback of *The Brothers Karamazov*. Now he was wearing a fur coat, a loose-fitting Russian peasant blouse and heavy boots. And I knew that there would be Stolichnaya vodka on the dresser in his apartment.

We sat through the however many hours of *Ivan* and later we went back to his apartment. He poured me a vodka and one for himself.

"What's in the box?" he asked.

"My book. What I've done of it. I was going over to see Mandy, but she wasn't home." I paused, not sure I wanted to do this. Then I took the plunge. "Do you want to take a look at it? I'd like your opinion."

Liam looked doubtfully at the box. "There's an awful lot of it," he observed.

"I've got all night." I got a bit defensive. "Look, if you don't want to. . . ."

"Okay, I'll read it."

The time that passes while somebody is reading what you have written is the longest time in the world. It is what prisoners call "hard time." I counted cracks on the wall. I washed dishes in the sink. I made tea in Liam's samovar. I peered out the window, watching a few people scurry by in the postmidnight cold.

For a while I tried sitting on the arm of Liam's chair and reading over his shoulder, as if somehow I could will a better reading of the words on the paper by telekinesis. But he finally looked around at me in annoyance, and wouldn't start reading again until I went away.

I moved over to the other armchair, and after awhile I fell asleep. I dreamed that I was in the operating theater of a large medical school. I was strapped on a table in the middle of the room, naked, spread-eagled. A bright light shone down upon me. A professor stood above me wearing a white coat and carrying a long pointer in his hands. He was lecturing to a packed house of students in the seats overhead. I couldn't see his face or the faces of the students in the amphitheater because of the brightness of the overhead light.

The professor's words were meaningless, a gibberish of nonsense syllables. As he spoke he illustrated his lecture by touching me with the long pointer—my breasts, my belly, my head and arms and legs. He used it to spread apart the lips of my vagina and to spread my cheeks to expose my anus. He touched it to my clitoris, activating a buzzer or vibrator that aroused me shamefully and brought me to a writhing show of passion that stopped agonizingly short of orgasm. There was no reaction, however, from the audience of faceless medical students. They sat attentively staring down at me, taking notes with their pencils on their legal pads.

The professor then proceeded to vivisect me. With the same pointer now suddenly turned into a scalpel he drew a bloodless incision down my front, opening my chest and belly. He scooped out my entrails and held them up for the scrutiny of the students. Their pencils scribbled away industriously. He then moved up to the crown of my head and touched the scalpel to my temple. And now for the first time I recognized the profes-

71

sor. It was Liam. And all of the students scribbling notes on their yellow legal pads in the bank of seats overhead were Liam.

And Liam the professor said, "Now, gentlemen, let us have a look at the brain. . . ."

I woke up in a cold sweat. Liam's chair was empty. The paper box was on the seat. The naked light bulb still burned.

I looked around for Liam and found him in bed, asleep.

I didn't wake him up. Nor did I undress and join him. I slept as I had been, curled up in the chair, fully dressed.

In the morning I awoke and made tea, then sat at the table and read through the manuscript in the thin morning sunlight. After awhile Liam got up. I heard him in the bathroom, taking a shower. I knew it was a cold shower from his snorts and gasps of shock.

He came out singing "The Song of the Volga Boatman." He was in his robe, toweling his hair dry. He had begun to grow a beard. He poured himself a cup of tea, stirred some jam into it, and joined me at the table. I ignored him. He tried making small talk. I refused to be drawn in.

"What is it?" he asked finally. "The manuscript?"

I looked at him. I sipped my tea and said nothing.

"Look, you were asleep when I finished. I didn't want to wake you up."

"I'm awake now."

"Well," he said, running an index finger down the stack of white pages, "it's really very interesting."

He paused, as my heart sank like raw meat in cold

oil. *Interesting*. The dreaded code word for nothing good to say. He went on, damning with faint praise, larding on a patronizing encouragement while I listened. I felt as if I were two people sitting inside a cardboard box looking out through a slit. One person was watching and listening to Liam, the other was looking around the room, counting the cracks again, impersonally browsing and itemizing to kill time.

". . . a very nice ear for dialogue in a couple of places," he was saying. Pompous fucking prig!

The pages on the table in front of me represented not just the work of the past few months. They represented my life, and my talent. They were drawn from notes that I had kept since I was sixteen. They were drawn from the experiences of a lifetime. Sure, it hadn't yet been a very long lifetime, but what the hell. Jane Austen wrote *Love and Friendship* when she was fourteen. Liam, ranting on about maturity and delicacy of image, was reducing those pages to so much novelty toilet paper.

". . . too heavy-handed in places, I'm afraid. You're going to have to learn that the stylistic imagination sometimes needs to take the oblique approach, rather than the obvious. Read Colette, read . . ."

"Fuck Colette!" I exploded. "This isn't Colette, this is me! If you don't like it, just say so. Who the hell are you, the goddamn *New York Review of Books*?"

He gave me an injured look. "You asked for my opinion," he said stiffly.

"And I sure got it, didn't I?"

"All right, it's great, it's brilliant. Is that what you want to hear?"

That was exactly what I wanted to hear. But not this way. I was close to tears.

"Hey, come on," Liam said. He got up and came around the table to me. He kissed my ear and the side of my neck. He slipped his hands down the front of my sweater to squeeze my breasts. "Let's not fight. Come to bed. I'm sorry."

His strong hands kneading my breasts felt good. He had been moody lately and we hadn't made love in over a week. I looked over at the bed and thought of the pleasure that awaited me there. Perhaps I was being unreasonable. I had asked him, he was right. If I couldn't take a little criticism. . . .

Liam felt the anger draining out of me as my body began to respond to his caresses. "Good girl," he praised, pinching my nipples lovingly. "No reason for us to fight over a little thing like this."

It was snowing as I walked back through the streets of the Village and SoHo to my bleak aerie above Broome Street. The first snow of winter. It had a serious look to it, as though it planned to stick. I myself had no such sureness of purpose.

I had been decisive enough ten minutes earlier when I had rocked Liam with a roundhouse slap to the face and staggered him backwards onto the bed, mast still raised expectantly through the front of his robe. For all I knew his angry cries of injured innocence as I slammed out of his apartment might have been real. I didn't much care.

A sanitation truck was on my street as I turned in, picking up the garbage. *There's imagery for you*, I thought. As I drew abreast of it I had a sudden impulse to take the cardboard box that contained my manuscript and chuck it into the dull devouring maw of the refuse collector.

I did not, though.

Chapter 10

Early in February Mandy's company gave a performance at the Beacon Theater on Broadway at Seventy-fourth Street. It would be my first opportunity to see her dance.

It had snowed ten inches a few days before, and then a thaw had come in. Dark snow lay along the streets and sidewalks in dead, decaying ridges. Slush-choked swamps spread like castle moats from the curbs out into midstreet. The daylight air was thick and grey and when night came the street lamps cut ineffectively through to light the city to a dirty pale yellow.

I took the subway to Fourteenth Street, changed for the express, and rode the three more stops to Seventy-second. When I came up from underground a fine drizzle was falling. I picked my way through the cold lakes that littered the street corners and made it at last to the Beacon.

In spite of the wretched conditions there was a good crowd on hand. It was Mandy's first New York concert in two years. People were lined up at the box office. Mandy had given me a ticket, so I went on in.

The lobby of the old theater was crowded with dance patrons milling about and calling out greetings to one another. I went into the ladies' room and got some paper towels to dry my feet, as my boots had sprung a leak. By the time I came out it was nearly curtain time, so I gave my ticket to the usher and went to my seat. It was in the fifth row of the orchestra, just in from the aisle. The aisle seat next to me was empty, but the rest of the orchestra was pretty full. I read Mandy's biography in the program and then the house lights dimmed and the curtain went up.

For the next forty-five minutes I sat entranced as Mandy and her company wove their magic on the stage. All the dancers—two other women and two men—were excellent, but Mandy clearly outshone them, infusing her movements with an extra dimension of grace and clarity. When she was dramatic, it was thunder and lightning; when she was ethereal, she floated transparent and barely brushed the stage; when she was sensual, the auditorium throbbed with the pulse of her passion.

When the curtain fell for intermission the audience broke into loud applause. I clapped till my hands hurt. It was only when the applause died down and people began to get up and head out to the lobby that I noticed that the seat next to me had been filled. I glanced over and saw a woman who was both stunningly beautiful and very familiar. Somebody I knew, surely, but I couldn't place her. I was not good with names. I had just decided that I had better say hello to her first, before she saw me, thereby putting the burden of recognition on her, when it suddenly came to me who she was: Susan Carraway. Susan Carraway, who that year was up for Best Actress for the film *Santa Fe*. Off screen, she was even more arrestingly lovely than on. Her lightly curled honey-blonde hair floated down around her shoulders. Her lips were a dark red, her skin was smooth and flawless. Her eyebrows arched over her most astonishing and most unforgettable feature, those two wide, slightly protruding blue eyes.

She turned and saw me staring at her. I blushed and looked guiltily away.

"Hi," she said. "You must be Sharon Clover."

"That's right."

"I'm not clairvoyant or anything. I'm a friend of Mandy's. She told me you'd be here. I'm Susan Carraway." She smiled and put out her hand. After a moment I had wit enough to shake it. "I just got into town this afternoon, and luckily she had a ticket for me. Isn't she fabulous?"

"Yes she is." *So are you,* I thought, but I didn't think it would be cool to say it. We chatted throughout the intermission about the program, the weather, the upcoming Academy Awards. She radiated warmth. She was one of the easiest people to talk to I had ever met. As the audience drifted back in, I was aware that people recognized her and wondered who I was.

After the show we went backstage to see Mandy. I moved self-consciously among the ropes and pulleys and flats behind the scenes, but Susan Carraway was obviously at home in those surroundings. With her as the featured member of our party we had no trouble being shown to Mandy's dressing room.

Mandy was drinking from a bottle of Gatorade and talking to Len Cuyler, one of the male dancers and Mandy's sometime lover. She greeted us. Susan Carraway and I sat in folding wooden chairs in her dressing room while Mandy finished going over notes and changing. Then the three of us went out for dinner.

We went to a Japanese place around the corner. Mandy and Susan ordered sushi. I wasn't in my element in a Japanese restaurant, so to play it safe, I followed suit. Twenty minutes later our waitress brought three little wooden platforms and set them on the table in front of us. Neatly arranged on each of them were strips of raw fish.

"Mine's a little underdone," I commented.

Mandy and Susan burst out laughing. "It's supposed to be raw, you ninny," Mandy said. "That's what sushi is. Raw fish. You've never had it before?"

"Oh sure, lots of times. Mom used to fix sushi all the time back in Minneapolis. She'd put it on to bake at about two in the afternoon. Sometimes Daddy'd grill it up on the backyard barbecue."

"I remember the first time I had sushi," Susan said. "It was when I first went out to Hollywood. My agent took me out for Japanese food. I didn't know anything about Japanese food. Raw fish, my God! But I couldn't let him think I was a hick, so I ate it. And wonder of wonders, it was good!"

"Well," I said gamely, "lest anyone here think I'm a hick. . . ."

I tried it. I dabbed a piece in a little of the green horseradish sauce that was dolloped on the platform, and popped it in my mouth. The texture struck me first, then the clean taste, and finally the powerful punch of the horseradish. It felt as if it were clearing a passage straight through the roof of my skull. It was wonderful.

"There," said Mandy, smiling. "Let that be a lesson to you, Sharon. Just like your mother used to tell us—never say you don't like something until you've tried it."

"Yes, Mom."

Toward the end of the meal I started sneezing.

"A delayed reaction to the *wasabi*?" Mandy asked.

"Nothing so exotic. My feet are wet." I sneezed again.

"We better get them dry before you come down with double pneumonia."

"Let's bring her up to my place," Susan offered. "It's just a couple of blocks."

"Oh please, don't bother . . . I can just—achoo!"

"She can certainly achoo, can't she?" Mandy asked.

"I haven't heard an achoo like that since Sandy Dennis."

"Come on, let's go."

The truth of the matter was that I was thrilled at the idea of seeing Susan Carraway's apartment. It is always fascinationg to get a peek into the private lives and surroundings of the famous. It was like walking into an issue of *People* magazine. I allowed myself to be bundled across the two blocks to Central Park West, through the gleaming brass doors held open by a solicitous uniformed doorman, into the spacious mirrored elevator manned by a genial, elderly elevator operator, and up the forty-odd floors to the penthouse.

"All right, swing into action," Susan declared. She tossed her coat onto a settee and kicked her boots into the corner. "You get her into a hot bath and I'll fix some kind of a toddy."

I left my leaky boots in the vestibule. Mandy led me into a bathroom that was roughly the size of my apartment, but not like my apartment in any other respect. The floor was separated from our feet by at least three inches of white fluffy carpet. The walls were papered with a delicate floral design. A beautiful art deco dressing table sat against one wall. The tub, the size of a small swimming pool, was sunk into a mirrored alcove.

Mandy ran water into the tub. A rich cloud of steam rose up, clouding the surrounding mirrors. I stood entranced, taking it all in.

"Better get out of those wet things," Mandy came over and helped me undress. I sat while she pulled off my pantyhose. "Mm, your feet *are* cold," she said. "Let me warm them up before you get into that hot water."

She rubbed my feet between her hands, then took them and put them up beneath her sweater against her stomach. "Ahhgh, that's cold!" I could feel the warm swells of her breasts against my toes. Susan came in with a tray of steaming mugs. "That looks like fun," she said.

"Warming her up."

"Good idea."

"They feel better now," I piped up. I was beginning to feel self-conscious, sitting naked in the plush upholstered chair while Mandy knelt between my legs, with my feet up beneath her sweater and my toes nestling her soft breasts. It was innocent, I knew; but it might not look that way to Susan Carraway.

I stood up and crossed to the deep, wide tub. The water was piping hot, so I eased in slowly. Mandy sat in the chair I had abandoned, sipping her hot toddy and watching me. Susan left the bathroom, saying that she wanted to change.

"How is it?"

"Delicious," I said.

"Feel better?"

"Much."

"It's a Jacuzzi. Would you like me to turn on the jets for you?"

"Oh, wonderful."

Mandy got up and pushed a switch on the wall. There was a low rumbling as the motor started and then the pulse of water swirled from the jets. "Ohh," I sighed, "perfect."

"Looks good to me," Mandy decided. "I think I'll join you." She crossed her arms and pulled her sweater up over her head, then slid down her snug leather pants. Her breasts were still small, as I remembered them. Her body was lean and sinuous, perfectly toned, flat across the belly and hollow inside the hipbones.

She tested the water with a toe and pulled back. "Hot!"

"You get used to it."

She squatted for a moment on the edge of the tub across from me. I was conscious of the fine pink slit of her cunt that was exposed to me. For a moment I was reminded of the exquisite sushi I'd tasted at dinner and found myself wondering what it would be like to run my tongue along that bit of pink. Blushing, I closed my eyes and leaned back against the rim.

Sharon

The underwater currents pounded against my hips, ass and thighs, sending a peaceful jangling through my body. I let myself relax totally and my legs floated up. A current found its way between them and stirred at the soft hair of my pussy. Unconsciously, I let my thighs drift apart. . . .

I say unconsciously. That is what I told myself at the time. I consciously told myself that I was drifting off, that the heat of the tub and the vibrations of the Jacuzzi jets and the vapors of the hot rum were robbing me of specific will. The eddies of the tub bore my body and arranged it according to their whim. It was all these things and no specific choice or wish of mine. I told myself this, I made this choice of choicelessness, because I didn't want to admit to myself the other currents that had begun to swirl within me. Something had happened to me the moment when my eyes had fixed on that delicate slice of pink nestled among the dark hair between Mandy's legs. It was a strange sensation. I didn't want to admit to myself that it was desire.

But it was desire. And I knew it. And so I floated in the tub, letting my legs spread apart in the churning waters, waiting. I knew I couldn't make the first move, but if Mandy did, it would be all right with me.

As ready as I was, I don't really remember when the caressing tease between my legs ceased being water and was replaced with soft fingers. The transition was so gentle, and the touch so liquid, that I moved from one to the other with only a vague heightening of the sexual arousal I already felt.

My eyes fluttered open. Mandy was in the water next to me. But it was Susan Carraway who was standing between my legs, stroking my fleece. I looked up at that face that was at the same time so new and so familiar. The smile, recognizable from posters and from the dark intimacy of movie theaters, was smiling down at me.

"Is this what you wanted?" she asked me.

I didn't answer. Her long fingers continued to tease lightly at the floating hair of my pussy. Every so often they would spray a little closer and skim the sensitive flesh of the lips, and a shiver of sensuality would course through me like an electric current. I looked up at Mandy. She put her arm around my shoulders, cradling my head against her hip. A smile passed between her and Susan.

"Then you don't know what you want?" Susan prodded. I knew, but I couldn't say it.

"All right." Susan moved away from me. She opened her arms and Mandy stepped into them. Their bodies, glistening with water and with steam, pressed together and their arms wrapped around each other. Their mouths opened, slowly drawing together, so that I could see their tongues exchange places just before their lips met and blocked the view.

They stood for a long time in the kiss. The water surged around them, bubbling at the smooth curves of the joined hips and the ripe mounds of buttocks. Mandy and Susan swayed gently as they held each other, moved either by a slowly rising passion or by the action of the water. They seemed to have forgotten about me. I watched them in their embrace and became intoxicated with the rich sexuality of the two women, one blonde and voluptuous, the other dark and lean.

They pulled apart at last. They lingered a moment in each other's eyes, their hands resting on each other's bodies. They turned at the same time and looked at me.

"Do you know now, Sharon?" Mandy inquired with a smile.

"Yes."

"What?"

So I was going to have to speak. I took a breath. The air itself was tangible with sex. Heavy drugged molecules of passion filled my lungs to bursting and sent a message coursing through my bloodstream to every extremity.

"I want you to make love to me."

They stood side by side now, naked hips touching, arms draped casually around each other. Mandy stroked Susan's breast. Susan leaned her head against Mandy's shoulder.

"Who? Which one of us?"

"Both."

They each reached out a hand to me. I took one in each of mine and Mandy and Susan drew me to them. Their arms met around my wet back. Susan's soft blonde hair fell on my neck. I could smell Mandy's sweet breath and feel the heat of Susan Carraway's brilliant eyes. It was Mandy who kissed me first.

We left the bathroom and went into Susan's bedroom. There was no light but the bright lights of the city at night that fell in through the picture window. We stood a moment, the three of us naked at the window, and looked down over the deceptively enchanted spectacle of Central Park at night. Each of its lampposts cast an eerie pool of illumination. Its roadways were a glittering, moving snake of auto headlights and a galaxy of tiny lights sparkled in the trees around Tavern on the Green.

We fell onto the bed. It was a wide bed, with the covers turned back and sheets of fresh-smelling linen. Susan took my face between her hands and began to cover it with kisses. I found her breasts, stroked and kneaded them. They were full like my own. The soft yielding feel of her flesh was wonderfully exciting, and as her nipples showed her pleasure by jutting against my palms I too began to squirm. Mandy slid down so that she was between us at waist level. She inserted a single finger into each cunt and slid in and out, slowly and experimentally. Then a second finger joined the first, and her thumbs found the two clitorises.

I heard Susan's sharp moan against my throat and I took her nipples between my fingers, pinching them. She cried out, moved her head down to my bosom, and seized my own rigid nipples between her lips. An uncontrollable quaking took hold of my hips and I rode hard against Mandy's hand. But Mandy, sensing that I was about to come, withdrew her hand. She took my thighs, pushing them as wide as they would go.

"Not yet, Sharon," she crooned. "It's too early for the first orgasm. We'll have many, but not yet."

Susan knelt beside her and they spread me, opening up my cunt. They leaned in and watched it quiver, near the brink of orgasm, unable to leap over the edge, but kept aquiver by the incredible close scrutiny of their eyes. When the spasms at last subsided, Susan bent her head down and flicked at my clit with the tip of her tongue, twice, stopping before I could gain the crest.

"Poor Sharon," Mandy commiserated.

"Are we torturing you?" Susan asked.

"Yes! But don't stop."

"No, darling. We won't stop." Mandy stretched

out on top of me and kissed me. I could feel the hair of her sex against mine, the lean cushion of her pussy pressing down on mine, her hard nipples losing themselves in my voluminous tits. Her tongue explored my mouth, ferreting out hidden pockets of sensation, knowing secrets that no man I'd ever kissed had known.

Susan's face burrowed in against our joined pussies and her hands slipped under my ass. She took hold of each cheek, her fingers plunging deep into the cleft between, and she lifted me up so that my clitoris was more exposed to the one that Mandy thrust down against me. At the same time Susan spread my cheeks and pushed her mouth against them. I felt the moist end of her tongue poke against the tight rear sphincter.

"No," I tried to say, but Mandy swallowed the word.

As Mandy's hard clit dug at mine, Susan's tongue made its way past the token resistance below and entered me. The two-pronged attack inflamed me to a new pitch and melted any inhibitions that remained. I flung my loins against the two women, wrapping my legs high around Mandy's back, opening my buttocks as wide as I could to Susan as she plunged the full length of her stabbing tongue into me. I began to sing a wild high song as the ecstasy took hold of me and this time I wouldn't give it up. My legs locked around Mandy's back, my hands found Susan's head and held her, and I came with such violent force that I nearly lost consciousness.

Through my gauzy awareness I knew that Susan and Mandy had fallen on each other, each with her head between the other's legs. I rolled over on my elbow and watched. Mandy was on her back beneath Susan. Her head was near me, and with her lips and teeth she was grazing gently on the blonde down that grew on Susan's pussy. She looked over at me and smiled, then raised her head and offered me her lips. I took them between my own and we kissed each other languidly until a furry brushing against our cheeks reminded us of Susan's impatience. We then turned our attention back to her.

Our tongues met and explored together the fragrant glistening petals of Susan's cunt. She squirmed and writhed against our probing and I became entranced with the sensuous movement of the round globes of her ass. I began to fondle them with my hand, feeling their firm texture and their supple smoothness. The shape delighted me. I had looked with enjoyment before at a girl's well-formed ass as it undulated in a tight denim package along MacDougal Street or moved in beautiful harmony beneath the flimsy camouflage of a bikini bottom at the seashore. But that had been a detached appreciation, as one would admire the form of a classical nude in a museum. Now the true sensuality of feminine buttocks occurred to me for the first time and I stroked them, marveling at their sheer erotic might.

Mandy was now concentrating on the distended point of Susan's clitoris, flicking it with machine gun bursts of her tongue. I pressed my lips against the writhing mounds of Susan's ass and rolled my hot cheeks against them. At the same time I sank my middle finger into the wet folds of her vagina. She twisted madly against it, drenching my hand. I moved my thumb up and found the small rear aperture that she had invaded in me. I didn't penetrate, but held it there tight against her, so that with each backward thrust she impaled herself upon it until it was buried fully within her. I could feel my thumb and finger touching through the narrow wall between Susan's two channels.

But I was ready now again and I didn't want my two lovers coming without me. I took my hand away and sat back. Mandy, seeing this and understanding, stopped too, leaving Susan teetering on the same precipice that I had been abandoned on before. She spun around, those famous eyes bulging wider than they ever had on screen, and clutched at her inflamed pussy.

"Oh no," she wailed, "*please*!"

Mandy smiled at me. "Have you ever wondered what it would be like to be a man?"

"Of course."

She leaned across the bed and reached into a drawer in the night table. She came back with a long artificial penis attached to leather straps.

"It's a dildo," she told me. "Put it on." Below us, Susan lay watching with her hands still tight against her crotch.

I took it from her. The shaft was of a hard rubber. Its feel was uncannily lifelike. Mandy showed me how to strap it on. A little bridge at the base ran back over my clitoris and nestled into my vagina. The long cock stood out from my pubic mound, half-comical, half-frightening. Mandy ran her fingers along it. I could almost feel them.

"Do you want her?" she breathed in my ear. She teased my nipples with her fingertips. "Do you want to take her like a man does?"

I couldn't speak, but I nodded.

Mandy stretched out alongside Susan. "What about

it, darling?'' Her voice was low, both coarse and honeyed. ''Do you want to be fucked?''

''Yes!''

Susan Carraway spread herself below me and I
knelt between her legs. The magnificent erection that
sprouted from my body became a part of my body. My
brain sowed nerve endings in its synthetic sheath, and
as the head touched and penetrated her I felt erotic
sensations sear through me. I was a man and I knew the
power thrill of piercing the soft body of a woman. But
I was a woman too, and I used that knowledge to wield
my weapon with a sympathetic subtlety that maximized
the pleasure that I dealt.

I stroked slowly, getting the feel of my instrument,
exploring the strange familiarity of a woman's cunt. My
hands moved over Susan's body, marveling at the
smoothness. She had gasped when I entered her; now
she lay back moaning in a semi-swoon. Mandy had
moved behind her and cradled Susan's head in her lap,
caressing the fair cheeks and the tousled blonde curls.

I leaned forward and increased the tempo slightly.
I took one of Susan's breasts in my hand and massaged
it. Mandy's hand moved to the other, matching my
caress. Our eyes met and we stared at each other,
smiling. An extraordinary intimacy was concentrated in
those few inches of air between our eyes. Below us a
singsong wail began to bubble from Susan's throat as
my thrusting found the delicate beginnings of her cli-
mactic rhythm.

I moved harder. Susan's hips began to thrash, her
whole body twisted beneath me. I rode her exultant,
pounding my loins against hers, filling her, piercing her
woman's core with my masculine power. Her center

leapt up at me in a spastic dance and she screamed as the first excruciating wave of orgasm broke over her, followed by another, and another, rising and then gradually falling away into a series of shudders and small, birdlike cries.

When Mandy and I made love it was slow and long, a meeting and tasting of lips and breasts and cunts and thighs. Susan lay spent and languid beside us, watching us, running a gentle hand over the flesh that was closest to her. Mandy and I were in no hurry. It had been acknowledged that the night was to be for our lovemaking, the three of us together. When Mandy was ready to burst I made her come with my mouth against her cunt. The sharp sweetness of her coming flooded me.

We put aside the dildo and brought each other pleasure with things that were totally feminine. For what seemed like hours we did nothing but kiss, stroke each other's hair and skin, lose ourselves in each other's eyes. We used fingers and tongues with women's wisdom upon women's bodies, knowing when to be gentle and when to be fierce, understanding and sharing in each other's needs and responses. It wasn't until the paling of dawn thinned the darkness over Central Park that I fell asleep, exhausted, with my head on Susan Carraway's soft bosom and my hand nested between Mandy's thighs.

Chapter 11

I went back to Liam after that. I was in a state of shock for a while. I didn't see Mandy. I put off having my telephone fixed. She wrote me several times, suggesting that we get together, but I didn't answer her letters. I spent most of my time at Liam's apartment, making love to him whenever I could. I had to reassure myself that I was not a lesbian.

Liam wasn't easy to live with. I never told him about my night with Mandy and Susan Carraway, but he had no trouble noticing my intensified devotion to his penis. He became rather lordly about it. Where before he had courted and been seductive, now he liked to tease me, to withhold sex as a punishment, to force me into acts I had previously refused to go along with. It was maddening. But I took it. I had to.

A false spring came, then an April snowstorm that bent the trees and buried the cars and brought out the children's sleds for a final go at winter. Then it really was spring.

Suddenly everything was in bloom. The trees burst into green, flowers opened overnight in the parks and in window boxes. The marijuana plant I was growing in my windowsill since February shot up two inches in a week. On the streets of SoHo young men and girls sloughed off their winter layers and paraded in shorts and open shirts. Outdoor cafes sprouted.

The SoHo galleries were shaking off the lethargies of winter and beckoning one and all to sample their springtime wares. Near me was a gallery called Venus Flytrap. It specialized in erotic art. The owner was a young Frenchman by the name of Blaise. He was having a big opening to feature the work of a woman who "did orgasms." I wasn't clear from that description whether she painted them, had them, or gave them. Blaise was a friend of mine, and although I wasn't an important person, I was invited to his opening.

I dressed counter to the occasion. I knew the place would be full of nubile girls in clear plastic halters and peekaboo bodysuits. There was no doubt in my mind that I could hold my own with any of them in the feminine charms department, but for reasons of personal style—call it aloofness if you will (some did)—I chose a more demure way of dressing: a white linen skirt, pencil-slim, and a white crèpe de Chine shirt unbuttoned to the valley of my bosom. To accent the effect I donned a pair of hoop earrings, and my one decent piece of jewelry, a pearl pendant that dangled between my tits in a way that couldn't help but direct attention to them. I did my hair and my make-up in a way to suggest both freshness and sophistication. I might not be an Important Person, but there was no reason why people shouldn't think I was. You never knew whom you might meet.

I had no trouble meeting people. It was knowing what to say to them that gave me anxiety. At a gallery opening the work on display was a natural source of conversational icebreaking. But when the focus of the work was orgasms, the ice was apt to melt somewhat faster than would normally be the case.

I arrived an hour late and the gallery was crowded. Blaise saw me and came over to kiss me on both cheeks.

"A good turnout," I complimented him.

"People like orgasms."

I laughed. "You may have hit on something there."

"Come. I show you around. If I see somebody important I have to talk to, you forgive me if I drop you like a hot potato."

The artist's approach was multimedia. Orgasms were represented in still photographs, celluloid, videotape, paintings, drawings, etchings, collage, papier-mâché, constructions, hangings and mobiles. Toward the back of the gallery, in the middle of the floor, was a large contraption that looked like a mechanical bull.

"The pièce de résistance," Blaise chuckled.

"What is it?"

"She calls it the Orgasmatron."

"Mother of God! What does it do?"

"Ah, but the answer cannot be given by description. Climb on top of it, Sharon. Then you will see."

"Why, Blaise, you dirty old man. I think you're trying to pull a fast one on me."

95

"Ma chérie, you have never allowed me to pull *anything* on you."

"Well, why don't we wait and let one of these other bimbos give the demonstration."

The mechanical apparatus was the center of attraction of the show. It was surrounded at this time by a couple of dozen art lovers. At least half of these were girls, most of whom were in the sort of outfits that I had previsioned in fashioning my own. A number of them were whispering to each other, or to their male companions, and giggling.

The artist was a woman named Stella Francis. She was in her thirties, a zaftig, blowzy woman with grey-streaked hair worn back and an olive green mechanic's jumpsuit unbuttoned to the waist. She was under the belly of the strange beast doing something with wire strippers and a screwdriver.

Eventually she slid out, mopping her sweaty forehead with a red handkerchief. "That oughta do it," she said cheerfully.

There was a round of applause. Stella Francis smiled at the crowd. "All right now, dears, who wants to have first go at it?"

"Go?" someone called out. "You mean come!"

Everyone laughed. It was that sort of crowd. But no one stepped forward at first. There was one girl I had my money on. She was wearing tight leather pants with great ovals cut out of the buttocks and a gold lamé shirt. She was with an older man who obviously wanted her to volunteer. He kept whispering to her and pushing her forward. But she didn't want anything to do with it and finally she started getting mad. She turned and wiggled back through the crowd, and I never saw her again.

While I was distracted by this bit of byplay another candidate stepped forth. She was a punk, pudgy-pretty with ghost-white skin and pink and purple hair. She had on a loose-fitting top of clear plastic perforated all over with a hole punch. Around her waist was an old automobile fan belt. Below it was a short knitted skirt. And beneath that, as far as I could tell, was nothing.

She looked back self-consciously at the area of the crowd from which she had emerged. Everyone was urging her on, and I couldn't tell which one or ones specifically she was with. Stella Francis took her hand and led her to the bull.

"Whaddaya think, it's gonna hurt? Believe me, sweetie, it don't hurt!"

"I dunno. . . ."

"Whaddaya think, folks? Is it gonna hurt?"

"No!" thundered the consensus.

"Well, you guys try it!" the girl retorted. But it was only repartee. Her eyes said she was ready to try the Orgasmatron.

"Now, this saddle, you'll notice, is specially constructed of eighty little nipples of hard rubber. When the Orgasmatron gets to shaking, those little fuckers'll start working on every little thing you got there to work on, honey." Stella patted the punk girl's plump ass. "So, you just grab onto this . . ." the saddle horn was a facsimile of an erect cock, about twice the size of the one I had used to act out my male fantasies on the sex goddess of the silver screen.

The girl took hold of the ersatz erection and swung

her leg up over the bull. Stella Francis tripped a switch and the monster began to shake.

The punk girl held on. A silly smile was still on her face. She mugged for her friends in the crowd and did a bit of burlesqued moaning. She shrugged her shoulders and made a little face, to indicate that the whole thing was a big put-on.

Then Stella Francis did something else with the hidden switch. The beast vibrated faster. The simpering smile on the girl's face was knocked askew. It stayed for a few moments more, but off center, jerked loose from its mooring.

"Speed!" Stella Francis announced, with a final twist of the knob. The Orgasmatron hummed like a monstrous hummingbird. The dildolike pommel moved up and down. The punk girl gasped and seized it with both hands, abandoning her skirt, which rose like a window shade until it rode high on her hips. The view below left no doubt that pink and purple wasn't the natural color of her hair.

Her pale flanks shook like salmon aspic. Gone from her face was any hint of superciliousness. Fast going was any hint of control. Her head flung back. Her eyes bulged out (again I thought of my conquest of big-eyed Susan Carraway that had left me so unsettled). A fleck of foam collected at the corner of her mouth. A strange low moan escaped her, cadenced but unbroken, rising gradually into higher octaves and decibels.

At last a shrill yelp let us know that the crisis had been reached. At the same moment the head of the pistoning phallus erupted, shooting up a bright bouquet of paper flowers. The audience, which had grown quiet, now broke into wild applause.

"She is a great artist, is she not?" asked Blaise, putting a congratulatory arm around the beaming Stella.

"That was really very impressive," I told her.

"Well thanks, sweetie. Say, would you like me to make you one? This one's sold, but I can do another on commission. Not exactly the same, of course. Each Stella Francis is an original. But at least as good."

"No thanks."

"Are you sure? I bet you have beautiful orgasms."

I hardly knew what to say. I thanked her, declined her offer, and moved off to mix with the crowd.

I was at the bar getting a spritzer when a man approached and started chatting with me. He seemed vaguely familiar. He was short and toadlike, with a bald dome and thick glasses. There was a gap between his front teeth you could have slid a quarter through. He was wearing a mustard gabardine three-piece suit. He wasn't my type.

"So what do you think of the show?" His voice was nasal and slightly effeminate.

"It's interesting."

"Don't like it much?"

"As a matter of fact, I do."

"See any orgasms you recognize, heh heh?"

No, but at this point I did recognize him. He was the man who had been urging the leather pants girl forward at the Orgasmatron. I was about to give him the brush-off when Blaise came over to us.

"Aha," he winked in my direction, "you literary people have found each other."

"Not exactly," the short man replied. "I haven't yet had the pleasure of an introduction to this young lady."

"*Eh bien*, let me be the instrument of such pleasure. Mr. Cohen, allow me to present Miss Sharon Clover, a most talented young writer. Sharon, may I present Mr. Joel Cohen, editor in chief at the publishing firm of Cartwright & Co."

Cohen held out a pudgy hand. "Enchanted, I'm sure," he said with a grin.

Perhaps he was not quite as short and toadish as he had looked at first. I took his hand and squeezed it. "How do you do, Mr. Cohen?"

"So, you're a writer?" He got his drink and we moved away from the bar to stand beneath a vinyl wall hanging that depicted a pair of spread female thighs centered with a puffy vulva. An ingenious electrical system within the piece operated a flashing red light in the clitoris and throbbing waves emanating outward like the ripples of a stone thrown in a pond.

I told him I was working on a novel.

"I'd like to see it," he said. "How far along are you?"

"I've got two hundred pages typed. About half, I guess."

"Send it over to me. Perhaps I can give you some guidance. Who's your agent?"

My heart sank. Of course I had no agent. And now he would dismiss me as a dilettante.

To my relief, it didn't seem to matter to him. "No matter. If you're any good, you'll have one soon enough. Just put it in the mail to me when you're ready." He took out his billfold and produced a business card. "Or better yet, drop by yourself. I'll take you to lunch."

*   *   *

As I was leaving the gallery I ran into Mandy.

"Sharon!" she cried. "Where've you been?"

"Around," I answered guiltily. "I've been busy."

She kissed me. I pulled away a little. She stepped back and looked at me. A smile tugged at her lips.

"I want to have a talk with you," she said. "Come, let's go get a drink."

We went to Odeon on West Broadway. It was a favorite place of Mandy's. It combined an air of newer-than-new with an art deco nostalgic feel. There was a long polished bar backed by a mirror of clean wood-framed curves and planes, globe lights of another era on the ceiling, large picture windows ruled into horizontal lines by white Venetian blinds. An electric clock was haloed with a neon nimbus that resembled the hair of the girl who had ridden the bull. Odeon was the new in place for the downtown art crowd. I had been there once with Zeb Toliver and he was there today. We said hello to him at the bar, where he was talking to a beautiful young man wearing a cream-colored necktie with a cream-colored shirt and no jacket. His name was David. They invited us to join them, but instead we took a table so that we could talk.

We ordered a bottle of California pinot noir. Someone came by who Mandy knew and she chatted with him for a moment. I looked out the window. It was a gorgeous afternoon. Two men walked by carrying a painting, a geometric abstract in bright colors. The waiter brought the wine, opened it, and poured a little into Mandy's glass. She was still talking to her friend, so I tasted it and gave it my blessing.

"You've been avoiding me, haven't you, Sharon?" Mandy asked me when her friend had gone.

It was a more direct question than I was prepared for. I blushed and stammered something evasive.

"You shouldn't, you know. You shouldn't be upset about what happened that night. That's what's bothering you, isn't it?"

"I guess it is."

"Didn't you enjoy it?"

I nodded. "I guess that's what bothers me."

Mandy grinned. "And now you're afraid of turning into a lesbian." She laughed. "Is that what you think I am, Sharon? A pervert?"

"No!"

"But it's not the sort of thing we were brought up to think of as good clean fun back in Minneapolis."

I had to smile. "No, that's for sure."

"But then, we also were handed a lot of garbage about sex in general, weren't we? Unless your mother was a lot different than mine. Your mother never struck me as much of a libertine."

"My mother never even told me where babies come from."

"I remember. I think I told you."

"When I got my first period I thought I was hemorrhaging or something. I had no idea what was happening to me. Alan Nobby had kissed me in the playground the day before and I thought maybe it had something to do with that. I was afraid to tell my mother. But she saw the blood on my nightgown. She got this weird look on her face and left the room. A minute later she came back with a box of Kotex. 'Here,' she said, 'I imagine you know all about this.' She dumped it on the bed and left. That was the extent of my sexual education at home."

Mandy refilled our glasses from the wine bottle. "So you've expanded your horizons quite a lot since you left the nest."

"Yes."

"You were a virgin when you arrived in Manhattan. God! I'm surprised the island didn't light up or tilt. And you were happy enough to get rid of your virginity, weren't you?"

"Sure. But that's . . ."

"Normal? With that dirty old man?"

"At least he was a man."

Mandy sighed. "Look, kid, there are different reasons for having sex. One is babies. If you're after babies, you won't get very far fucking Susan Carraway—or even me, though I hate to admit to any limitations. Another is duty, if you get yourself hooked up in that kind of a relationship. Sometimes you can use it to get what you want—sleeping your way to success, that sort of thing. That's okay, if you do it right. But the best one of all is pleasure. Sex is fun. You've noticed that?"

I confessed to have done so.

"Sex brings pleasure. That doesn't necessarily mean that pleasure is always sexual, or that sex is always pleasurable. But I've always taken it to mean that any sex you do get pleasure from is bound to be a good thing. I get pleasure out of fucking men and I get pleasure out of fucking women." She smiled warmly and touched my hand. "I got a lot of pleasure by fucking you."

"Well, I guess when you put it that way. . . ."

"Eating pussy doesn't make you a lesbian, Sharon. Look at Zeb over there. Just because he likes a cock in his mouth, does that necessarily make him gay?"

"I guess not."

"Of course in Zeb's case, it happens that he *is* a screaming faggot."

"I see," I said, laughing. "But not *necessarily*."

"You have grasped it perfectly. Sex is sex. Some things feel good, some don't. Some things that don't feel good still can turn you on. Try everything. If it turns you on, hey. . . ."

"You're right. I'm sorry I've been acting like such an idiot. I guess part of my head was still back in Minnesota. To tell you the God's honest truth, what we did that night turned me on like crazy. The trouble was, it also sort of scared the shit out of me."

"I know. But I didn't want to let it come between us. If we make love again or if we don't, it's okay with me. But I'd hate us not to be friends."

I felt terrific about myself for the first time in a long time that night when I went home. There was no need to go to Liam's place and grovel seductively, trying to get him to fuck my brains out just to prove to myself that there was nothing wrong with me. I wasn't a freak or a deviate. I was just a normal, healthy American girl. A particular kind of healthy American girl, true, but not a bad kind, as far as I could see.

To a writer, every experience is valuable. That night with my two lady lovers was something I would always have to draw on. It had enriched me in ways that I couldn't have absorbed in any other manner. The soft interchange of feminine parts and caresses had brought me a fuller understanding of what it is to be a woman. And my metamorphosis into a man as I strapped on that surrogate penis and mounted the gorgeous blonde wet dream fantasy of every American male had given me rare insight into masculine feelings and mentality.

Besides—there was no denying it—it had been a powerful sexual thrill. Pleasure, Mandy had shown me, was the measure of right and wrong in sex. The apple in the Garden of Eden was not temptation or original sin or forbidden knowledge or whatever they had taught us in Sunday school. The serpent's insidious gift to the human race was guilt.

I was twenty-one and I felt very lucky to have learned that already. If it turned out to be true.

Chapter 12

Practically speaking, any new insights into the philosophy of sex that I might have made were irrelevant over the next six weeks. During that time I threw myself back into my writing with a single-minded dedication that blocked out most social contact. I sat down with the manuscript and read it over with a large red pencil in my hand. At first I was in despair. It was hopeless drivel. Liam had been right. No, Liam had been flattering.

Gradually I managed to work my way out of the black hole of self-criticism into which I had plunged, to discover rays of light. The manuscript by now resembled the skin of a flagellant, criss-crossed with livid red stripes. Adjectives, sentences, paragraphs had fallen beneath my merciless pencil. Banalities had been routed, clichés had been put to flight. Whole pages of asinine dialogue were muzzled. Descriptive passages heavy with schoolgirl poetry felt the sting of my new, harder mood.

What remained, I decided, had a chance. It was honest and straightforward, drawn from life. I had taped into my notebook a favorite quote taken from the great nineteenth-century economist and journalist Walter Bagehot:

The reason why so few good books are written is that so few people that can write know anything. In general an author has always lived in a room, has read books, has cultivated science, is acquainted with the style and sentiments of the best authors, but he is out of the way of employing his own eyes and ears. He has nothing to hear and nothing to see. His life is a vacuum.

I wouldn't fall into that trap. I was writing of something I knew well: my growing up in the Midwest. My novel was set in Minneapolis in the early seventies. My heroine, like myself, was a tomboy turned artist. To avoid making it seem too autobiographical I made her a dancer rather than a writer. I had read once in a magazine the stern warning of some crusty New York editor to aspiring writers: "Never write in the first person and never write about writers." Two more traps that I was able, forewarned, to skirt.

By the middle of June I was ready. The two hundred pages I had started out with had been revised beyond recognition. The novel was still at the approximate halfway point, but I felt that this would be a good time to show it to Mr. Cohen at Cartwright. Gabby Lazare had assured me that editors like to get hold of a book before it's finished. It gives them more of a chance to mold it, she said.

This time I did not show it to Liam first. If my ego was to be shattered again, at least the hammer would be swung by a professional. I picked up the phone and with damp fingers I dialed the number on the card that had been tacked up over my desk, an icon to inspire me when the spirit was weak.

A secretary fielded my call.

"What is it in reference to?"

"It's personal," I replied. What else could I say? *I'm writing a book and I want Mr. Cohen to take a look at it and tell me if it's any good?*

"Just a moment." Suspicion thinned her voice. "I'll see if Mr. Cohen is in."

A long moment of Muzak, soft crackling strings playing a syrupy arrangement of Lennon and McCartney's "Paperback Writer" and then, miracle of miracles, Joel Cohen came on the line.

"Of course I remember you," he said. "Ready to show? Excellent. Let's have lunch."

I was no longer the innocent described in the earlier pages of this memoir. I remembered how Joel Cohen had looked at me at Venus Flytrap. I didn't deceive myself that a plump fortyish matron would have received the same attention that I was getting. It was my good fortune that I had sex appeal to offer. That was the lure. But I was hoping that my writing would be the hook.

We lunched at a dim hideaway on the East Side. I lugged along my manuscript in its paper box, tastefully concealed in a Fiorucci shopping bag to lend a little class. I had some naive idea that he would read it right then and there as we ate. I was quickly disabused of that notion. As I entered the restaurant and stood there a moment, blinking to accustom my eyes to the grottolike darkness, I realized that any reading beyond the large type on the menu would be totally impossible.

The restaurant was decorated to suggest a bit of African jungle—the sort of jungle that has floors thickly carpeted in red broadloom, chairs of upholstered leather that sigh and embrace you when you sit, surfaces that gleam darkly with a polished intimacy and sweet music that powders everything with its soft sugar.

We lunched on lobster bisque and veal cacciatore and talked of a variety of things that had nothing to do with literature in general or my book in particular. I sensed that it was considered indiscreet to raise the business of a business lunch while one was eating. Joel Cohen talked with some authority about marlin fishing and the pleasure boat he kept in the Florida Keys.

Finally, when the waiter brought the little plastic tray with the editor's American Express card back for a signature and he still hadn't broached the subject, I decided it was time for me to speak.

"I've brought my book."

"Oh?" He smiled and looked blank.

"My book. The manuscript of my novel—well, my half-novel. You said you wanted to look at it."

"Of course I do. You must bring it by sometime."

"I have it here." I lifted the Fiorucci bag.

"Wonderful." He took it. "I'll read it over the weekend."

It was only Monday. My face fell. "No sooner than that?"

He chuckled. "You are an impatient little thing, aren't you? A little word of wisdom, my dear: in this business you count yourself lucky if you can even get your agent to read what you've done within a month. When someone tells you he will read it over the weekend, you must never assume he is even talking about the coming weekend."

I was crestfallen. "Oh," I said dejectedly. "I see."

He patted my hand. "Don't worry about it, Sharon. I will read it this weekend. In fact, to hold me to it, why don't you come out to the Hamptons? We've got a house on the beach and an empty guest room. I'm sure my wife would enjoy your company."

"Oh, I couldn't." My heart pounded wildly. The Hamptons! The summer mecca for the New York literary crowd. And a houseguest of the editor in chief of Cartwright!

"Of course you could. It's settled, then."

In those sun-favored days that stretch between Memorial Day and Labor Day, the world of New York's arts and letters drifts east with the instincts of migrating birds to settle on the beaches and byways of a handful of little towns toward the farther reaches of Long Island. Those fortunate ones whose lifestyle permits it make the trip just once each way—out in May, back in September. For the regularly employed, it is a twice-weekly struggle on Friday and Sunday evenings.

Midtown Manhattan to midtown East Hampton is a jaunt of just over two hours in a fast car on an empty road. But on Friday evenings, with twenty million cars all funneling over the same bridges and tunnels, cramming onto the same highways, creeping around the same disabled tractor-trailers, the trip can take somewhat longer, anywhere from three to six hours or more.

Ours, highlighted by a spectacular geyser that erupted from the radiator cap, took five and a half.

It was dark when we got there. I peeled myself, sweaty and crumpled, from the leather seat, hoisted my stuffed weekend bag, and followed Joel Cohen up the steep slope of the entrance walk to his door.

Mrs. Cohen emerged from the living room as we came in. She had a gin and tonic in her hand. Mrs. Cohen was a vehemently blonde woman in her early forties. Her face was very tan and somewhat weathered, not especially attractive but well maintained. Her figure, which was largely visible in shorts and a halter beneath an open hostess robe of lavender silk trimmed with gold was a tribute to Dr. Herman Tarnower.

Mrs. Cohen greeted us with charm that was laced with the suggestion that her husband was somehow to blame for the lateness of our arrival. I did not, however, feel any hostility or suspicion directed at me. I was relieved that she didn't seem to suspect that there had been (and there certainly had not been) any hanky-panky along the way that was responsible for our delay.

She took me under her wing.

"Hi," she said. (She pronounced it "Hoy." Beyond that I won't try to reproduce her manner of speech, except to say that it was distinctive.) "You look bushed, honey. Joel's not exactly the world's greatest driver, is he? Come on now, let me show you your room and let you freshen up a little."

"Thank you, Mrs. Cohen."

"Mrs. Cohen? That's my mother-in-law. Call me Molly."

She took my bag and put an arm through mine with an "us girls" intimacy. We left Joel Cohen blink-

112

ing owlishly in the entrance hall and climbed a flight of
stairs that were garlanded with heavy fisherman's ropes
and nets and hung with large plugs of cork. My room
was simple and pleasant. Through the open window I
could feel the sea breeze and hear the waves murmuring
somewhere in the darkness against the sand. I showered
away the sweat and grime of the drive and came down
changed and refreshed. We spent a pleasant, chatty
evening drinking gins-and-tonic, nibbling on cold mac-
aroni salad. I saw to it that Joel Cohen had my manuscript with him when we all retired for the night.

I half-expected a nocturnal visit from Cohen: even,
possibly, one from Molly. But my sleep wasn't dis-
turbed. I woke up in the morning to the smell of salt air
and frying sausage.

The view from my window was spectacular. I was
perched above a dune, looking down over smooth,
sun-bright sand to water that rolled away forever. It was
my first encounter with the ocean.

I went downstairs and breakfasted with Molly.
Cohen was still asleep, so my gnawing anxiety about
his reaction to my book couldn't be satisfied for the
moment. I went out and walked on the beach, swam in
the cold water, lay in the sun and read.

When I returned to the house it was nearly noon.
Molly was downstairs with her hair in curlers as I
entered.

"Hi. How's the water?"

"Fine. Isn't Mr. Cohen up yet?"

"Oh yeah. I sent him into town to pick up some
things. We're having some people over this afternoon."

* * *

A few hours later the deck outside the Cohen house was filled with people come alive from the pages of the Sunday *Times* Book Review. George Plimpton was there, Carl Bernstein, Bill Henderson, Gail Godwin, Nancy Milford, William Buckley, Meredith Rich— people whose work and reputations were magic to me. Kenneth Rhymer, a bearded playwright whose latest, *Two-Thirds of All the Rest*, was a smash that season at the Public Theater, was there with a slight poetess from North Carolina named Leslie Hollister whose work I hadn't read, but had heard much discussed. William Shears, best-selling author of the Ward Bobb thrillers, lounged against the railing talking to an ample blonde woman who was an editor at a literary magazine.

Cohen introduced me around as his "new discovery." I glowed. He hadn't yet told me privately what he thought of my manuscript, but it was evident from his introduction that he had been favorably impressed. I was making valuable contacts and becoming absorbed into the group that would one day constitute my peers.

Molly had told me that it was going to be an afternoon party, but a group remained as the sun flattened and then disappeared below the horizon. Below us on the beach a few Frisbees still floated through the air, a few children still dug in the sand until parental voices called out through the dusk and summoned them home.

Our party was now much smaller. It was composed of the playwright Rhymer and his ethereal, white-faced poetess, the gangly Shears and his large-bodied lady, whose name was Lee Evans. Completing the picture, of course, were the Cohens and me.

As the dark brought breezes off the water to cool

114

the air the ladies donned wraps, and finally we all moved inside. The living room was a sunken floor off the patio. Wide comfortable sofas made a squared-off U facing a small stone fireplace. The floor was covered with a soft fur rug made in patchwork from the pelts of many different animals. The walls were built-in bookcases crammed to overflowing with books. Where there were spaces of plain wall, they were filled with large banal canvases of seascapes, painted by Molly.

A stack of records went onto the stereo and Joel Cohen built a fire. Joints went around. Drinks were refilled. A glass vial that contained a white powder was passed. People dipped a little spoon that was attached to the cap of the vial into the powder and snorted it into each nostril.

"What is it?" I asked Lee Evans.

"Coke."

I tried it. It hit the back of my nose with a burning impact, then exploded into my brain. There was a pleasantly bitter taste, then a cool, wonderful lift.

The talk turned to the old days. For the three men and Molly, apparently, they had been days spent in common.

"Remember Goltz? He had that coffee house near the Circle in the Square? He used to fuck all his waitresses in that little office he had off the back area where the folk singers used to play. But I mean that office, it was just about the size of a broom closet, you had to do it standing up if you were going to do it at all. So one night he had this chick in there who was really roasting his chestnuts. And what's-his-name, that twelve-string player from Virginia . . ."

"Corley Winfield."

"Yeah, Winfield, he was out there trying to play 'Bill Bailey Won't You Please Come Home,' and there's this rattling and moaning going on behind that door, and Winfield, he tries to ignore it for a while, and he tries to play over it, and finally he gives up. He puts down his guitar, he stands up, and says into the mike, 'Folks, I get the feelin' I ain't the main event around here. Let's bring on the real stars of our show . . .' "

"Oh yeah!"

"And he snatches open the door, and out tumbles Goltz and that waitress, humping away like dogs in the road! She's got her dress up around her shoulders and he's got his pants down at his ankles. There they are in the middle of the stage and Goltz can't stop."

"He kept fucking?"

"He sure did. Right there on the floor, and the whole time he's cussin' out Winfield in that heavy German accent of his: 'Vinfeelt, you bastard! You neffer vork here again! You are fired! Ahhhhhhh! Ohhhhh! Yes! *Yes!* Yes!' "

Several jugs of wine had found their way into the center of the floor. We filled our glasses and sat on the sofas or on the fur rug. I listened to story after story of the escapades of the great and colorful characters of another era, from the lips of people who had known them and had been there. The English couple, both famous poets, who would bake one white bean and one dark bean into the dessert custard. The guest who got the dark bean bedded the husband, the white bean got the wife for the night, with no regard for the sexes involved. A tragic story of a young dancer who threw herself naked to her death from the apartment of her lover, a well-known journalist and novelist, when he

116

stayed out for several nights with another woman. The anecdotes kept coming and I, the junior member of the gathering, listened with silent attentiveness and an aching nostalgia for a period I had never known.

"Ah, they were a lusty bunch," Cohen said.

"What do you mean, they?" Shears demanded.

"Yeah, and what do you mean were?" Lee Evans chimed in.

"Still plenty of lust in these old loins," Rhymer declared.

"Oh? Let's see." The dark-clad poetess at his elbow turned and unbuckled his belt. Molly leaned over and helped her slide off his corduroy pants.

His penis lay flaccid on its side like a little rodent surprised in its sleep.

"Some legends are best left undisturbed," Leslie Hollister remarked wryly.

"You caught him unawares; he'll grow," the playwright protested.

" 'Therefore think him as a serpent's egg,' " Shears intoned, " 'which, hatch'd, would, as his kind, grow mischievous, and kill him in his shell.' "

"Well, Bill, if we're quoting Shakespeare. . . ." Lee Evans shifted her bulk for a closer look at Rhymer's dormant member. "How about this: 'I can suck melancholy out of a song as a weasel sucks eggs.' " She smiled up at Rhymer. "As You Like It, Act II, Scene V." She lowered her head into his lap.

Rhymer sighed and a beatific expression settled across his face. " 'Her lips suck forth my soul,' " he said. "Or something very much like that. Christopher Marlowe, Dr. Faustus."

I couldn't believe it. Not two feet from me, her

117

wide bottom looming toward my face, an editor of a leading literary magazine was giving head to one of America's leading playwrights. And everyone was quoting classical drama. It was bizarre.

But of course, this was just the sort of thing they had been talking about. I had been sitting there feeling sentimental about the colorful, free-spirited days I had missed. And now here they were, right in front of me.

"Let's get Lee a little more comfortable," Molly suggested.

Lee was wearing a large, formless beach dress that unzipped most of the way down the back. I helped Molly unzip it and we pulled it off her. Underneath Lee had on white cotton panties and a bra.

"I'll get the top, you get the bottom," Molly decided. I moved back to the wide white expanse of cotton and peeled down the garment. Lee's enormous pink ass filled the room.

"Magnificent," breathed a voice at my elbow. It was Cohen. He ran his hand over the fleshy mountains. "What a spectacle!"

Leslie Hollister came around to look. "Very nice," she agreed. "Does anyone have a belt?"

"A belt?" I asked. "Why?"

"To stripe her a little."

"You can't!" I was shocked.

"Of course we can. Look at this pussy." Critically, she poked a finger into the blond puff that showed between Lee's buttocks. "Hardly wet. A shot of leather will lubricate that nicely."

Strangely, there was no protest at this talk from Lee, who surely must have heard it.

118

Cohen stood up and removed his belt. "I'll do it," he offered.

Leslie took the belt from him. "No," she said, "Not you." She held it out in my direction. "You."

"No! No, I won't."

"There's nothing to it. Just swing. You can hardly miss."

"Go on, honey," Molly urged.

"Give it a whack, Sharon," said Shears. "Don't worry, she'll love it."

I was the callow youth, the apprentice in this room full of literary stature. And once again I was acting like the scared virgin, the little small-town girl. I tightened the belt around my hand and pulled my arm back. With more force than I had intended, I brought it around.

Whack! The flat leather resounded off the smooth pink of Lee's ass. It quivered and a moment later a soft red mark appeared, the width of Joel Cohen's belt. Lee's face didn't move from Rhymer's lap.

"All right," Leslie said. "A couple more warm-ups and then start in for real."

"You mean harder?"

"That's what I mean."

I brought it back again and struck. Strange feeling, to stand above a kneeling woman wielding a leather strap against those wide and willing cheeks. Another soft stripe appeared, and in the yellow silk below I saw the beading of a few glistening drops of moisture. It was turning her on!

I hit harder. Her ass was undulating now and her head was pumping faster in Rhymer's lap. From the expression on his face I could tell that Lee's lips were picking up the tempo. I began to feel a tingling in my own body as I applied the lash. Red lines covered nearly all of the vast expanse of Lee's ass and upper thighs, as if she had been sun-bathing in the nude beneath open Venetian blinds.

Leslie took the belt from my hand. "I think that's done the trick, don't you?" She inspected the vaginal crevice with her finger again. "Perfectly wet," she pronounced, licking the moisture from her fingertip.

"Then what the hell are we waiting for?" Cohen exploded. He ripped off his trousers and his boxer shorts, then tore his shirt up over his head. His body was squat and covered with hair. His cock was already erect. Like the rest of his body it was short but thick. He crouched over Lee's striped and writhing ass, one hand on each cheek, and plunged down into the damp blonde moss.

"Come on, Bill," Molly said to Shears. "We've gotten our beautiful young guest all hot and bothered, and now we're neglecting her."

"Oh, that's all right," I said lamely. But he was already unbuttoning my shirt, while at the same time Molly tugged down the zipper at the side of my brief red shorts. A moment later I was naked. A step away the Carolinian poetess watched, arms folded in frail amusement.

"Honey, you do have the most gorgeous red hair," Molly exclaimed, running her fingers through my pubic thatch. "I would've sworn it was out of a bottle. My God, Bill, isn't she a looker!"

"You certainly are," Shears agreed, gallantly including me in the conversation. "And I think we are being extremely rude remaining dressed in the presence of such sheer naked beauty."

A rasping cry to our left announced that Rhymer's resistance had come to an end. I saw his body go rigid and his face flush dark beneath his beard. Lee's mouth burrowed hard against him, while Cohen bounced away at her rump. A moment later the playwright slumped to the floor as Lee knelt over him, swallowing contentedly.

Bill Shears took me in his arms and kissed me, with the same brawny assertiveness with which Ward Bobb addressed the women in his enormously popular books. I felt his hard member imprisoned flat against my belly. Then from behind I felt Molly's arms encircle us and felt her wiry bush grind up against my ass and her soft tits mash into my shoulder blades.

They began to move against me, at first slightly out of sync and then in unison. A fever of arousal caught hold of me and I bit at Shears' lips and moved my pelvis up against his cock and back against the pussy that pressed behind me.

Another presence entered our fray. At first I was baffled by what seemed to be disembodied fingers pulling at my hard and throbbing clitoris, a phantom tongue sliding up into the grateful darkness of my cunt. Then I freed my head a moment to glance downward and saw Leslie crouching among our legs. The slim, fragile poetess had dropped her clothes on the sofa behind her and was kneeling bare-flanked and bare-breasted in the forest of our twisting legs, reaching up with face and hands to the centers of our passion. She moved fluidly back and forth among the three. Then her hand slid in between my belly and Bill Shears' and withdrew his imprisoned erection. With the sureness of a skillful seamstress threading a needle, she inserted it into me.

As Shears began to fuck me I arched my head

backward and received the mouth with which Molly
avidly sought me. Her lips enveloped mine, her tongue
invaded me. It was extraordinarily long. It reached to
the back of my throat and I nearly gagged, but I ac-
commodated it. I fastened onto it with my lips and
sucked it. I could feel her respond with her pussy,
driving its rough tangle deep between my nether cheeks.

Fingers—perhaps Shears', perhaps Molly's, I was
beyond discerning—squeezed at my nipples and I began
to moan into Molly's mouth and felt her answering
moan. Bill Shears' breath was coming in hard grunts as
he pumped up into me, knees bent and driving, while
beneath our thrashing bodies the pale poetess darted,
penetrating every available orifice with fingers and with
tongue.

When Shears came he let out a roar and his final
rigid thrust lifted me off the floor and held me there.
Airborne and impaled I shuddered against him, vibrat-
ing rapidly into a climax of my own. Shears buckled at
the knees and we sank in a heap to the floor. I lay back
and rested my head on the luxurious pillow of Lee
Evans' bottom, watching while Leslie Hollister and
Molly Cohen finished their business nearby.

Chapter 13

I spent much of that summer disporting with the literary crowd. Often it was at one or another of the Hamptons. Sometimes it was as a guest of the Cohens, sometimes with other writers and publishing people. It was not all one long orgy, as my experience on that first weekend might have suggested. But it was hardly a celibate summer.

I was still seeing Liam. In fact we were getting along much better now. My newfound entree into the writers' world had raised me greatly in his estimation. Liam knew a number of the same people I was seeing now, and many of the writers who were his drinking companions confided to me the same vague sense that Liam was a real talent and that his book, when it was finished, would be something important.

I still hadn't been granted so much as a peek at the title page. I knew, or believed, that there were mountainous stacks of typing paper covered with double-spaced type in Liam's locked closet, but he wouldn't even reveal to me the location of the key. Though I was not, like Bluebeard's wife, inclined to snoop.

Liam remained a wonderful lover. My sexual carryings-on with aging literary lions only served to reinforce this fact. I was bowled over at first, both literally and figuratively, by my new intimacy with America's men and women of letters. But after a bout in bed humping some balding, paunchy Pulitzer Prizewinner or stroking the slackening flanks of a middle-aged lesbian short-story queen, I was glad to return to Liam's firm young body and indefatigable cock. If he wasn't always tender or sensitive, he was tireless and generally willing.

As the summer wore on and I still had no commitment from Joel Cohen about my book, I began to grow uneasy. He had read it, finally. He was encouraging. He gave me suggestions as to how to rewrite it. I followed them. He read it again, and was encouraging again. But there was no move toward a contract.

Through my new contacts I did succeed in finding an agent. Her name was Nanette Marx. I went to see her on a July afternoon when the rest of the world was at the seashore and the city lay suffocating in a haze of moist heat. I arrived early at the building and sat outside on the stoop, waiting and watching the people come and go. A pregnant woman and her husband passed me and went in. She would have outweighed him by a good twenty pounds even without her swelling stomach. She had perspired through the white sailor-suit maternity dress she was wearing and the whole topography of her belly showed, down to the distended navel and the blue traces of veins. They were arguing and she seemed to blame her husband for the discomfort she was experiencing. Very likely she was right.

A few minutes later another pregnant woman arrived, then three more expectant couples. There seemed to be something in the air. I stood up and dusted off the back of my dress, wondering if it was possible to get pregnant from germs after all, as I had believed in second grade.

It was time for my appointment. I entered the lobby and searched for Nanette Marx's name on the bank of buzzers. I discovered, to my relief, that there was a Mrs. Bing who taught natural childbirth also in the building. One mystery cleared up.

Nanette Marx's office was next door to her apartment. A male secretary in shirtsleeves and a bow tie met me at the door and showed me back. Nanette Marx was hanging up the phone as I walked into her office. She came around her desk to greet me. She was in her middle thirties, I guessed, a long-faced woman with large healthy teeth and heavy-lidded eyes that slanted up toward her nose. She was wearing a mumu and was barefoot.

"Hello," she said. "You're . . ."

The phone rang. She dashed back around her desk and grabbed it. I waited, unsure of whether to sit or stand. I opted for standing, finally, since aside from Nanette Marx's wooden swivel chair, there was no place to sit. It was a disheveled room, with every surface stacked high with books and manuscripts. The view from the window was of rooftops. In the distance between buildings was a razor-thin sliver of the Hudson. Nanette Marx kept chatting, occasionally looking around to see that I was still there and wiggling her fingers at me in a sort of apologetic salute. It sounded as though she was talking with somebody who had something to do with the movie business. I wasn't unduly impatient. I would have hoped that soon she would be similarly voluble on my account with Hollywood's money men.

At last she hung up. But she'd no sooner reached the words: "I'm sorry. Now, you're . . ." when the telephone rang again. It was like this for the entire afternoon. I was with her for two and a half hours and in that time we spent perhaps ten minutes talking. The rest of the time Nanette Marx was on the phone.

But when I finally left her office she had assured me that she was very interested in me.

"Bill speaks very highly of your work," she told me, referring to the novelist friend who had given me her name. "I'm looking forward to reading it. I'll try to get to it over the weekend."

Liam was impressed. "Nanette Marx? She's supposed to be pretty good."

I waited by my phone almost constantly for the next week. When friends called I would cut them off peremptorily. I turned down lunch dates, even though I was broke and could barely afford Campbell's soup at home. I didn't fool around with Liam when he came over during the day. I couldn't risk a voice husky with sex and heavy breathing when The Call came.

But Nanette Marx never called.

Ruefully I recalled Joel Cohen's words at our first lunch. "In this business you count yourself lucky if you can even get your agent to read what you've written within a month."

The second week I couldn't take it any longer. I called her.

"She's on the phone," Wayne, her secretary, told me. "She'll have to get back to you."

And so the agonizing process was extended for another week. And another, and another, as my calls went unreturned.

And then she did call.

"Sharon, it's Nanette. How are you doing? Look, how'd you like to write a sexy Gothic?"

"A what?"

"You know. A Gothic. The girl running away from the old house. With a little bodice-ripping tossed in."

"Nanette, what about my novel?"

"Haven't had a chance to get to it yet. I'm going to try to tackle it this weekend. What about it? The advance is twenty-five."

"Twenty-five hundred?"

"My other phone's ringing. I've gotta have an answer. How about it, Sharon? You want it?"

Want it? How could I possibly want it? But I took it. Twenty-five hundred wasn't much, but then neither was what I had in the bank.

"A Gothic?" Liam was a study in contempt. "You're going to write a *Gothic*? Why not peddle your ass on the streets?"

I had thought of that, too. But other friends urged the logic of this route upon me.

"You might as well be professional about this, Sharon," Mandy advised me. "You're a writer. So write. A lot of good writers have hacked for a living during the hungry spells. Look, when I first came to

New York the big philosophical question among all the acting students I knew was whether they would ever do a commercial. They'd argue it endlessly—would you if it was a really classy production? A great director? A product you believed in? A hell of a lot of money? Perish the thought! Last month I was up seeing a producer friend at an ad agency and I ran into four of these guys at a call for a spaghetti sauce commercial."

"But that doesn't mean they were wrong before."

"No. It just means they weren't hungry before."

I called Gabby Lazare. She had been a vocal idealist in the writers' group, to which I had not been now in some months. I wanted to see what her opinion would be.

"Can I stop over and see you tomorrow morning?"

"Sorry, Sharon, I can't. I'm working on a piece for the *National Enquirer*."

A tempestuous wind drove the rain in horizontal sheets across the greensward. It was black as night, though the Seth Thomas clock in the hallway had just struck four. Jennifer sat and counted the deep-throated, reverberating chimes. Her hands trembled on the fine Wedgwood cup and saucer that she held forgotten, the tea grown cold. Her heart struck in time with the chimes of the clock and kept striking after the last low chime had rolled away into stillness. And still Gardner had not come home.

There was a sharp unearthly crackling that went through her like a shower of pins and a bolt of lightning lit the grey park below her window to a pallid brilliance. The tremendous boom of thunder that exploded on top of it shook the house, rattled the windows and the china in the cupboards, and drowned out Jennifer's terrified scream.

For that brief, bloodless flash of light had revealed the figure of a man coming toward the house.

It was not Gardner.

She leapt from her chair, sending the frail cup crashing into pieces. Dark tea spread like a bloodstain across the white carpet. Jennifer let out a cry of dismay, but she did not pause in her headlong flight toward the door.

Down the stairs she flew! Along the marble corridor, her footsteps hammering like the wild beat of her heart. There was the door. Her fingers closed around the cold brass knob, fumbled for the key. . . .

The handle tore from her grasp with a wrenching jerk. The door flew open. And there, dripping with dark rainwater, was Lamont.

"You!" she gasped.

"Hello, Jennie. Aren't you going to invite me in?"

"No! You've got to go! Please, go, now!"

Slowly he shook his head. His black hair was plastered in tangled curls across his wide forehead. Water collected in glistening beads at the ends of his bristling mustache and fell past white teeth exposed in a merciless grin. His currant eyes burned into her eyes, into her soul.

"Not this time, Jennie. You're not turning me away again."

"Gardner—he's here. He's upstairs. He'll be down in a minute."

"Gardner's on his way to Boston. His plane couldn't land. The Carrandale airport's closed, all flights have been diverted. He won't be here till tomorrow." He

129

stepped inside and swung the door shut behind him with a hollow slam. "That gives us tonight, Jennie. All night."

Jennifer's hand flew to her mouth. She backed away from Lamont in terror. "It's not true," she protested, "you're making it up . . ."

Outside the sky lit up again with another vivid burst of fluorescent light. A thunderclap like a death knell rent the air. Lamont was telling the truth, Jennifer knew. No plane could land at Carrandale Airport in a storm like this.

He walked slowly toward her. Her eyes, involuntarily, dropped to his midsection. She gasped. There, outlined in the soaked fabric of his trousers, monstrous and swollen against his thigh, was the unmistakable evidence of his desire.

"What . . . what do you mean to do with me?" she whispered.

A low, mirthless chuckle rumbled from his throat. "Everything."

She ran as if death itself, or something worse, were after her. Through her frightened tears she cursed Gardner for ever bringing her to his old family mansion in Carrandale, and cursed him more for bringing around this wild hunter, Gardner's boyhood friend who had grown into a friendless and untamed savage. She darted up the service staircase, down a hall, and ducked into the east bedroom. There was a key in the lock! She turned it and leaned against the door, sobbing and panting.

There was a telephone on the night table. She ran to it and picked it up. There was no dial tone. Franti-

cally she jabbed at the cradle with her finger, but the line was dead and could not be revived.

With a silky, sickening creak, the wall panel next to the bed swung open and Lamont stepped through.

"I know this house like the barrel of my gun," he drawled. "Wonderful maze of secret passages. There's been lots of romantic intrigue in this room over the years, Jennie. A worthy tradition to follow in."

He walked toward her, and she knew now that there was no escape. She screamed and slapped him hard across the mouth. A pencil line of blood appeared at the corner of his lips. He smiled.

"So you want it rough, do you, Jen?"

His hands went to the collar of her blouse. With a savage motion he ripped downward. The soft cotton was rent asunder, and she was naked to the waist. Her full bosom heaved beneath his stare.

"No!" She backed away, looking desperately for something she could use to keep him at bay, something she could use as a weapon. Her eye fell on a vase of pussywillows by the window. She had picked them herself, just the day before, after Gardner had driven off. She snatched up the vase and heaved it at Lamont's head. It struck off his temple, and he staggered.

It was now or never! She made a dash for the door—and his hand closed around her ankle, bringing her crashing down face-first across the old four-poster bed. In a flash he had sprung upon her. He bound her hands with his necktie and tied them to the head of the bed. Then with the sashes from the curtains he tied her legs, spread-eagled, to the posts at the foot.

"Little wildcat," he said in her ear. "We'll see what it takes to tame you."

131

With his hunting knife he cut away her belt and her skirt; then she felt the cold steel blade slip beneath the elastic of her panties.

"No!" she cried again, but she knew that she could no longer hope to stem his insatiable tide.

The sharp blade sliced through one side severing the elastic; then the other side, and the silken garment was drawn away. With her legs spread wide apart and tied, she knew her most secret parts were now exposed to his impudent gaze.

She heard again his low, merciless chuckle.

"Pussywillows, eh? You wanted to do me in with pussywillows? Well . . . let's see if there's any truth to the old saying, 'what's sauce for the pup is sauce for the pussy.' "

She lay there trembling, not knowing what he meant, but knowing that it would be as useless to ask for information as to beg for mercy. She pressed her face against the eiderdown comforter and waited.

And then she felt a soft tickling against the naked flesh of her buttocks. It continued until she looked, and saw him standing over her, trailing the long bunched stalks of the pussywillows along her rear.

"That's right, Jennie," he said pleasantly. "They're soft, aren't they? Pussy-soft. But they can also sting!"

With a sudden motion he drew the willow stalks back and lashed them hard across her tender skin. "Oh!" she cried, as the thin stalks smarted against her. His hand came down again, and the flesh of her bottom began to burn under the furious whipping. She cried, and begged, and twisted against the bonds that held her as Lamont continued to thrash her defenseless derrière. Her buttocks writhed, and rose, and suddenly

132

*the tenor of her cries had changed, and the rolling of
her hips had taken on the tempo of desire.*

*"Oh yes!" she cried, turning her head toward
him. "Hurt me, Lamont! Take me!"*

*He flung the scourge of pussywillows aside. His
hands tore at his belt and he cast away his clothing.
His gleaming member stood out, awesome in its dimen-
sions and its urgency. Jennie's eyes widened with hungry astonishment; compared to Lamont's mighty oak,
Gardner's was a mere sapling. She knew at last that
this was what she wanted, had always wanted.*

*She knew at last that this was why she had come to
Carrandale . . .*

They loved it. They wanted me to do another. I
refused. They offered to up the ante by another thousand. I was tempted.

Liam ridiculed the idea. "No amount of money in
the world can pay the price of selling out," he told me.
He was wearing overalls these days and drinking a
cheap whiskey he called "hooch." He was disdainful
of wealth. He wouldn't patronize the local A&P—the
"company store," he called it—and instead ate at my
apartment almost every night.

"Writing that trash, Sharon, you're selling your
soul. Of course, maybe a fella ain't got a soul of his
own, but only a piece of a big one . . ." I had noticed
John Steinbeck's *The Grapes of Wrath* in his overall bib
pocket the last few times Liam had come over.

I talked it over with Mandy. I had always found
her advice to be sound.

"How long did this one take you?" she asked me.

"About two months, maybe ten weeks."

"Figure you get it down to two months. And they're offering what now?"

"Thirty-five."

"Let's say you get it up to five eventually. Assuming you can keep turning the crap out at full speed, that's a peak rate of thirty grand a year."

"Less Nanette's ten percent."

"Twenty-seven grand. But you're not going to be able to churn it out week in, week out. Let's call it four books a year. That's twenty thousand . . . okay, eighteen, less the agent's commission. That's assuming Nanette can keep 'em coming as fast as you're ready to do 'em."

"Yes. I see what you mean."

"I don't mean anything, Sharon. I'm just trying to lay it out logically. But I guess it's not really a logical issue."

"No. I mean, they're easy to write, but . . . it gets pretty embarrassing when you're at a party with all these literary types and they ask you what you're writing. It's like being with a bunch of nuns and explaining that you give blow jobs for a living."

"Hmmm. So meanwhile, what's happening with frog-face and your real book?"

"Joel," I said that weekend on the deck of his East Hampton house, "what's the story with my book? It's been over four months now. Look," I cast an expressive hand out toward the nearly deserted beach, where a couple strolled in hooded parkas while their golden retriever gamboled in the surf. "The season's over. It's fall, summer's gone, the frost is on the pump-

kin and the wolf is at the door. I need an answer. I've
got to sort out my life.''

"Well," he said, beginning the familiar hedge,
"as you know, I think the work shows a great deal of
talent. You have a good ear and a solid grasp of the
fundamentals of good writing. A real sense of . . ."

"Cut the crap, Joel." This was Sharon Clover,
lately of Minneapolis, Minnesota, the lint of a cross-
country Trailways bus still clinging to her clothing, the
flat "a" of a Midwestern accent still flavoring her
speech. But I had paid some dues at least, I felt. I had
taken a lot from this man, even if he was the editor in
chief at Cartwright & Co. I had had enough. "Are you
going to publish it or aren't you?"

He looked at me, eyes darting behind his thick
glasses, hunting for a way out. There was none. He
sighed, and puckered his mouth in a sheepish smile.
"I'm afraid not," he said.

I had been expecting that response, I thought, but
it still hit me like a blow to the stomach. I tried not to
let it show on my face.

"Why not? If you don't mind my asking."

"It's . . . it's just not our sort of book. It's not
really hard cover."

"Oh boy." I could've pursued it. I could have
tried to pin him down, to make him squirm, but my
heart wasn't in it. I knew the decision had been made
for months. Possibly since even before he read the
manuscript. All I was likely to get now was more of the
same publishing world shorthand gibberish: *it lacks
tension, it's plot-heavy, there's not enough plot, too
many (too few) characters, it lacks a central point of
view, it doesn't speak to me.*

"Then all of this out here has really been a bit of a fraud, hasn't it? Just a cute trick to let you and Molly and your friends bang the little broad from Minnesota."

"No, Sharon," Cohen replied uncomfortably. "It hasn't been like that at all. You're our friend. You're practically one of the family!"

"Which one?"

"I beg your pardon?"

"Never mind." I got up. I felt very tired and dangerously close to tears. The early November wind rustled the dune grass, and I pulled my sweater close around my chest. "Good-bye, Joel."

"Where are you going?"

"Back home."

"Back to Minnesota?"

I laughed. "No, back to New York. You haven't beaten me down that badly yet."

"I wish you'd stay."

"I bet you do. But I'm going."

He stood up and came over to me. He put his hand on my arm. I lifted it aside.

"If you won't change your mind, let me drive you to the train."

"No need. I'm taking a cab."

"All right. I'll call one for you while you pack."

"I'm already packed. And there's a cab waiting for me in the driveway."

He followed me through the house to the front door. My blue duffel was sitting there, packed and ready. In the driveway the cab driver slumped behind the wheel, reading a newspaper.

"You weren't kidding."

I shook my head and picked up my bag.

"How did you know what I'd say?" he asked me.

"Oh, come on, Joel."

"What if I hadn't? What if I'd told you we were taking it?"

"I'd have sent the cab away."

I slung the bag over my shoulder. "So long, Joel," I said. "Don't think it hasn't been fun."

I walked down the driveway. The driver sat up and put on his cap as I got in.

"Let's go," I said. "The station."

He started up his engine and we pulled around the driveway's little loop. Joel Cohen was standing in the doorway looking rattled. As we pulled onto the road, Molly Cohen's gunmetal Mercedes slowed down for the turn in. She peered at me through the window of the cab. I waved.

Chapter 14

Going out in New York on a Sunday morning for the *Times* is one of the most satisfying rewards of city living. It's not just the *Times* itself; it's the going out that's important too, and the Sunday morning. People who take home delivery miss half the fun.

There is the walk to the newsstand through a neighborhood still drowsy with the aftereffects of Saturday night. Huge piles of newsprint tower toward the sky. You slip out a paper from somewhere in the middle of a stack, to be sure of getting one that isn't thumbed and torn. Hefting it in one hand, you flip through the sections to make sure they're all there. You check the dots at the top of the front page—four dots is the code that insures that you're getting the latest edition. Only then do you place your money on the counter and start home, feeling the pleasurable weight of the huge journal tugging at your arm.

If you are serious about your Sunday *Times*, you have to wait until Sunday to get it. There are people who argue passionately for Saturday night, but they are wrong. In the first place, the news is that much less current. The sports section knows less than you do of the important Saturday afternoon and evening encounters. Wars could have been declared, leaders assassinated, politicians compromised, banks robbed, airplanes hijacked, children kidnapped, rockets launched, crooks caught, jails broken, embassies bombed, and you would never be the wiser.

To the journalistic connoisseur, the words "city edition" are as cheerless as the words "individually wrapped slices" to a lover of great cheese. Beyond that, Saturday night is not the proper time to read the Sunday paper. Coming home late from movie or party or disco, a person is not in the right frame of mind to sit down with as weighty a commitment as *The New York Times*.

"Yes, but we'll read it in bed in the morning," some argue, and so it sits there, a presence in the apartment, intrusive, not yet accepted. Out of a vague sense of uneasiness or guilt a section is picked up, a few paragraphs or pages flipped quickly through, not much, but enough to take the edge off its enjoyment in the morning. And through the night it lies on a chair or a tabletop, bulky and pale, its freshness already beginning to decompose.

But rules are made to be broken, and on that Friday evening when I rolled back into Manhattan on the train fresh from my stylish exit at the Cohen beach house, I went to a newsstand that offered a Friday

sneak preview edition of the Sunday *Times* and fur-
tively took one home with me. I wasn't interested in
late-breaking news and sports. I wanted it for the
classifieds.

It was time to look for a job.

I might or might not be a talented writer. Opinion
on that seemed to be divided. Nanette Marx finally had
gotten around to reading my manuscript. She'd been
lavish in her praise. "I'll sell it in a week," she had
assured me. But it hadn't gone in a week, or a month.
As one publisher after another turned it down, (often
with lovely encomiums: "The bitter truth is, Nanette,
that this is just too good for our market," one note
read) Nanette noticeably lost interest and once again
became unreachable by phone. When I turned down the
second erotic Gothic, our relationship drifted away.

And there were bills to pay. I was two months
behind on my rent, I owed Mandy five hundred dollars,
my phone had been cut off, and I came into the apartment every evening and flipped the light switch with no
real confidence that the lights would still go on.

Liam came over on Saturday morning as I was
going through the want ads, circling listings with my
red pencil.

"Get something with an airline," he suggested as
he buttered my last English muffin with my last bit of
margarine. "That way we can get discounts on plane
fares."

"Are you sure you wouldn't like me to get something in a restaurant?"

"No, that's okay. If you were a stewardess you
could bring back those little meals on trays. Mmm—
plastic-wrapped ham and cheese sandwiches . . . Salis-

bury steak under foil . . . and all those little liquor bottles, too.''

"Sounds great. Why don't you do it? They have stewards too, you know.''

"Not me. It would take away from my writing.''

But on Monday my classified section with its red-ringed job targets went into the wastebasket. On Monday morning I got a call from Joel Cohen. His conscience had been bothering him, he said.

"Does this mean you're going to publish my book?''

"No, I'm afraid not. But I'll tell you what I will do. I'll give you a chance to see how tough it is from this side of the fence.''

And so the following Monday morning I began my career as an associate editor at Cartwright.

My first inkling of the toughness of life on the other side came with the rush-hour subway ride to work. There was not too bad a crowd when I got on the Lexington Avenue IRT at Spring Street, but by the time we pulled away from Fourteenth the car was packed. I had a seat in the middle of the car. A strap hanger in a loud, loose-fitting business suit loomed over me with his face buried in a copy of the New York *Post*, and at every sway and jolt of the train his crotch lurched within inches of my face. I couldn't be sure whether it was by accident or design, but there was no mistaking the erection that jutted out against the red-and-gold plaid.

At Grand Central there was a mass exodus, including my admirer. I began to think I might get a chance to breathe again for the one remaining stop, but before the exiting passengers were off, a new crowd had begun to elbow its way onto the car, causing a traffic jam and some angry words at the doors. By the time I realized that I was going to have some trouble reaching those doors when we got to Fifty-first Street, it was too late. I rode all the way to Bloomingdale's before wriggling through the compression of bodies and popping out onto the platform.

Faced with the choice of taking the downtown subway back to Fifty-first or running down Lexington, I chose the latter. I arrived at my new job five minutes late, a bedraggled shell of the carefully put together career girl who had left SoHo forty minutes earlier.

My office wasn't as grand as I had expected. My idea of what an editor's office should look like was based on old Doris Day movies and one visit to Joel Cohen's office. I knew I shouldn't expect one comparable to his, a grand and spacious arrangement on the downtown corner of the Cartwright Building, commanding a view of most of Manhattan below Fifty-third Street. But I had hoped for a window. I later discovered I was considered lucky to have landed an office at all, rather than one of the partitioned cubicles outside.

Across the hall from me was a young editor named Duncan Childs. He came over at coffee break time to welcome me to the fold.

"I have no idea what I'm supposed to be doing," I told him. "Nobody's said anything to me yet."

"That is known as a state of grace. If you just sit in here very quietly, maybe no one will say anything to you until Friday. Then you can pick up your paycheck and sneak home with nobody the wiser. If you can keep it going long enough, people will start assuming that you're doing something secret and important and they'll

leave you alone. As the years go by you'll get raises
and profit sharing and become known as 'The Mole of
the Thirty-seventh Floor.' "

"That's easy for you to say."

"On the contrary, that was very difficult for me to
say. I'm generally the shy, silent type. You seem to
draw me out."

Duncan Childs was easy to like. Physically he
resembled Woody Allen, with thinning, frizzy hair and
thick glasses. He wore baggy chinos and a blue work
shirt with a yellow wool necktie. His most frequent
facial expression was a self-deprecating smile accompanied by downcast eyes.

He filled me in on what to expect. "Mostly you'll
be giving second readings to manuscripts that editors
have looked at and want another opinion on. After
awhile you'll begin to develop your own sources and
bring books in. If you find something you really believe
in, Cohen will shoot it down. It's an exciting career for
a young woman fresh out of Vassar with a summa cum
laude degree. Are you such a young woman?"

"No, I'm a young woman not so fresh out of
Minnesota with a failed writing career."

"There are no failed writers, only lousy books. As
you will have plenty of opportunity to see around this
place. Good luck."

Joel Cohen called me just before lunch. He sounded
smug. I knew he expected me to fawn over him for
giving me this job and it annoyed me.

"Welcome to the fold," he said.

"Thanks."

"Getting adjusted?"

"Pretty well, considering nobody's given me anything to do. Are you sure you told them I was coming?''

He chuckled. ''Don't worry, you'll have more work than you know how to handle. Meanwhile, while you're still feeling grateful to me, how about lunch?''

I told him I had a date. I lied, but I had made a decision: from now on, my relationship with Joel Cohen was going to be strictly business.

Liam seemed pleased by my new employment. With my first paycheck we went out to dinner to celebrate. We ate at a little Italian restaurant where the food was cooked and served by the couple who owned the place. There were only a half dozen tables in the room. We brought our own wine and they opened it for us and brought us glasses.

''What are you reading these days, Liam?'' I could tease him about his chameleon literary suggestibility, but only a little. It was apparent that we were out of the Steinbeck phase. The overalls had been gone for some time now and had been replaced by a bohemian elegance of dress (black velvet jacket, loose white shirt, flowing neckerchief) which was matched by an impulsive elegance of speech.

''I? Why I've begun reading Lawrence!''

''T.E. or D.H.?''

''D.H.''

''*Lady Chatterley's Lover*, I hope,'' I said, thinking ahead to the end of the evening. What with one thing and another, we hadn't made love in almost a week.

''No.'' He shook his head. ''I've started with *Women in Love*. What a wonderful book! It seethes and twists like a serpent, ribbons of silver entwined with darker currents of dissolution.''

I sipped my wine and smiled. It had been years since I'd read *Women in Love*, but I remembered it as a book filled with sensuality and passion. The wine was good and it spread its warmth through me as I drank it, letting it carry the sexual warmth of anticipation with it, building up in my body against the promise of an evening that was still very young.

After we finished dinner I was ready to go home or up to Liam's apartment, but he wanted to stop for a drink. We went to the Lion's Head and had cognacs. Geoff Norton-Taylor was there and he joined us. Geoff was a writer for one of the news magazines. He was a swarthy, heavyset man of thirty-seven. I had met him several times with Liam. Once while Liam was off at the men's room he had asked me to go to bed with him. I didn't like his timing or his approach and I turned him down.

"By God, Geoffrey! We haven't seen you in eons!"

"I've been away on assignment. A piece on Sumo wrestling in Japan."

"Sumo wrestling!" Liam's eyes lit up. "That's something I've never seen."

Geoff shrugged. "It was pretty interesting."

"What's it like?"

"Well, it's pretty hard to demonstrate in here. . . ."

Fifteen minutes later we were up in Liam's apartment. Liam and Geoffrey moved the furniture back against the walls, leaving the rug clear. I made myself a drink—whiskey with a splash of seltzer from a syphon that stood on the bureau top—and sat on the edge of a chair.

"Now, how is it done? Show me how to begin."

"These are pretty big guys, remember. They stand like this. . . ."

"Wait. We should strip, shouldn't we? To do this properly?"

Women in Love began to come back to me. I remembered now that not all the sensuality that seethed through the novel had involved a man and a woman.

Liam and Geoff undressed. Geoff seemed to pause when he reached his briefs, but Liam showed no such delicacy. He flung away his clothes without hesitation and Geoff quickly followed his lead.

Physically they were much like Birkin and Gerald in the book from which Liam was playing out his scene. Liam was Birkin—slim, alabaster-skinned, a poet's body, all the less substantial-looking in contrast with Geoff's brutish Gerald. Geoff's skin was coarse and ruddy. His shoulders were thick, padded, matted with hair that covered most of the rest of his body as well. His wide forehead and wider jaw gave him almost a caveman look. Now, as he crouched naked, arms looping forward in his Sumo stance, he looked capable of breaking Liam in half with a single twist.

In the original version, it was the frailer Birkin who had the expertise in jiujitsu, which brought things to an even pass. Here Geoff was the expert, which made it a mismatch of potentially tragic proportions.

Liam imitated Geoff's crouch, as Geoff began to explain the rudiments of Sumo technique. The only area in which Liam appeared to have a clear-cut physical superiority was in sexual equipment. Liam's cock swung down between his legs, at least three or four inches long even unerect. Geoff's was a thick stub half-lost in

147

the bramble of his pubic hair. Only the hooded, uncir-
cumcised head poked out.

Geoff made a sudden move and Liam was on the
floor on his back, blinking.

"You okay?"

"Yeah . . . that was fast." He picked himself up.
"Let's see it again."

The second time Liam parried the move better,
successfully bringing Geoff down with him. They grappled on the floor, got up, came together again. From
time to time they would stop, panting, while Geoff
explained the theory of this or that grip or move. Liam
was a quick study. His eyes glowed with enthusiasm.
Soon their bodies began to gleam with sweat.

Liam had a greater quickness than his opponent.
He soon mastered the moves that Geoff taught him, and
they were matched fairly evenly after about ten minutes. They grappled, came together, fell, twisted away,
drove into each other with a fierce enthusiasm that
totally enveloped them. I was forgotten. At that point I
might've been somewhere else. I watched the sweaty
limbs strain against one another, and the muscles gleam
and bulge. I felt myself responding sexually to the
naked maleness of it. Unconsciously I found that I had
begun moving back and forth against the arm of the
chair that I was straddling.

Geoff found an opening and seized Liam around
the waist, lifting him and swinging him to the floor.
Liam twisted and caught Geoff's leg, bringing Geoff
crashing down on top of him. They lay there for a long
moment without moving. I was afraid Liam might have
been hurt.

"Liam, are you okay?"

But then I did see movement. They had fallen with Liam on his back and Geoff reversed above him, his head down between Liam's knees. As Geoff slowly raised himself by his arms, I noticed that Liam's cock was beginning to extend and point upward, until it came to within a few inches of Geoff's rugged jaw.

Geoff was watching it too. He seemed hypnotized by that pink sightless eye. His tongue ran uncertainly across his lips. Then Liam rolled away and sat up, putting his hand across his erection to conceal it. Geoff crouched next to him. His cock was hard as well, jutting forward. Both of them were breathing heavily. Liam seemed the more embarrassed by the evidence of sexual desire, perhaps because I was there. He looked at me.

"Why don't you join us and try some of this?" he asked. "You could learn something too."

He wasn't talking about wrestling. He wanted to make love to Geoff and he felt uncomfortable about doing it without the buffer of a woman to take the sting out of the homosexuality. I didn't mind. I had grown almost intolerably horny as I watched them grappling each other naked. The sight of their sudden awareness of their own desire for each other had already caused me to drench my panties and the padded arm of the chair with an orgasm.

"All right," I agreed. I stood up and stripped off my clothes.

The two men stood and faced me. Both cocks were at full extension. Their eyes glistened. They didn't look at each other, but I felt their eyes meet through mine. I was the conduit. Their sexual energy traveled through me, discharging in either direction with redoubled strength.

"Show her that spin-and-drop."

"Right." Geoff approached me. "So, Sharon, I come at you like this . . ." He grabbed my waist between his big hands and turned me gently to the side. "And then you do this . . ." He showed me a maneuver with my leg. We tried it in slow motion and wound up on our knees.

Our faces were in direct line with Liam's stiffened cock.

"Oh my," I said. "Look at this!" And I took it in my mouth. I sucked on it for a few moments, sliding it deep inside me. Often I could lose myself in this act, but this time the circumstances were different. I kept a sidelong eye on Geoff, watching the hunger grow on his face. His bear paw came up and began stroking Liam's groin, while his other hand massaged my back. When I was sure he was ready, I took my lips away and pointed Liam's glistening sex toward Geoff's mouth. Geoff's lips opened and he swallowed it like a hungry bird devouring a worm.

I reached down between Geoff's thighs and found his erection. It was so thick I had difficulty wrapping my fingers around it. I began to stroke it in and out. The cadence of his whisker-roughened face against Liam's groin quickened. I turned my eyes to Liam's face. His eyes were closed and his lower lip caught between his teeth.

With my other hand I reached around and fondled his ass. The cheeks were clenched tight. I stroked and squeezed, gradually insinuating my way into the cleft. I found his asshole and worked my middle finger up against it.

His eyes shot open. He looked down at me.

"You like to do me there," I whispered up at him. "How'd you like to try it?"

He shook his head convulsively. "No!"

"Oh, sure. . . ." I pressed up with my finger, gaining entry. "You like that, don't you? There's nothing wrong with it, Liam. I make love to women, don't I? You don't think there's anything wrong with that. It's an experience. Writers need to try all kinds of experience."

He still shook his head, but less emphatically.

"How about it, Liam? Geoff wants to fuck you. You'll never be more ready for it than you are right now."

Geoff had withdrawn his head and was looking up expectantly now at Liam. Liam's cock twitched, swollen and unattended. Neither man spoke. The negotiations, so to speak, were in my hands.

I gave a final stroke to each of them, then I lay down on the floor beneath Liam. I spread my legs open wide. "Eat me," I crooned. My fingers played with my wet pussy. "Kneel down and eat me."

With a groan he dropped to his knees and fastened his lips to the lips of my sex. He didn't flatten himself on the floor, but knelt with his ass sticking up in the air.

"On the kitchen counter, Geoff," I murmured. "There's butter in the butter dish. It's soft."

Liam drove at me with tongue, lips and teeth, with a fervor that he had never equaled before. I came once before Geoff returned from the kitchen, five steps away.

151

Geoff knelt behind Liam and applied the warm butter to the crease between his cheeks. Then he raised himself up and drove forward.

Liam's head snapped up from my crotch with a cry of startled pain. "Ahhh! No!"

He tried to wrench forward, but Geoff caught him around the neck with the crook of one elbow and grabbed his scrotum with the other hand.

"Easy, Liam," he said hoarsely. "Just give it a minute."

Liam's eyes were wide and his head jerked like a wild horse with a saddle on his back. After a moment Geoff gave a slight thrust. Again Liam tried to buck, but Geoff's double grip kept him pinned. After a bit, Geoff began to move again. He was moving rhythmically now and Liam was no longer trying to dislodge him.

"Sharon," he cried desperately, "come here!" His face was contorted with anguish and passion. "Get under me!"

I turned around and backed in under him until I felt the hot rubbery pole of his cock butt against my flanks. Then I reached back and took hold of the blind instrument, bringing it to the slick opening of my cunt. Liam surged into me with tremendous force, so that I had to brace myself hard with my hands against the floor to keep from being knocked flat on my face. I could hear the slap and feel the jolting impact each time Geoff rammed into him. It was as if both of them were coming into me, a single extended male being united with itself in a spliced continuum of passion. Above me I heard Liam's voice raised in a lupine cry.

*   *   *

152

Sharon

Perhaps that evening was the beginning of the end of my relationship with Liam. He was never quite the same with me after that. We stayed together for a few months longer and we had a lot of good sex in that time. But there was something furtive about Liam from that point on, something guarded and self-conscious. It was as if in his most bravura fucking he was not simply reveling in our mutual pleasure, as he once had, but trying to show me something. Trying to show me he wasn't gay.

The thought never really occurred to me. I had found the experience a tremendous turn-on, just as a lot of men get off on watching two girls going at it. I never thought any less of Liam for that. But it bothered him.

The real rift that finally drove us apart came later. And that was something much more serious. That was something very serious indeed.

153

Chapter 15

In the months that followed, Joel Cohen's prediction proved to be accurate. I was swamped with work. As soon as the editorial staff of Cartwright & Co. discovered I was there, endless stacks of manuscripts were deposited on my desk. From the door, my desktop resembled the skyline of Manhattan done in paper.

At first I was overwhelmed by the avalanche of paper. Then slowly I began to dig my way out from under it. I arrived at the office every morning at seven-thirty and worked till six, taking lunch at my desk. When I left, I took a manuscript home with me. I took my work to bed with me. Liam was amused for a while. He delighted in reading over my shoulder and making withering remarks about the quality of the writing. Soon the novelty of that wore off and he resented the intrusion of several pounds of paper into the arena of our passion. That resentment often took the form of goading him into volcanic sexual activity, sending any number of manuscript pages back to the offices of Cartwright & Co. with suspicious sticky substances on their crumpled surfaces.

My new job was a powerful aphrodisiac of sorts in another quarter as well. Nanette Marx, who had been about as easy to reach as Greta Garbo during the waning stages of my free-lance writing career, was now as chatty as Rona Barrett. In some mysterious way the news of my employment at Cartwright wafted across to West Seventy-ninth Street almost before my seat was warm. Hers was the first call on the new black telephone that was installed on my desk.

"Sharon! It's Nanette!"

"Nanette who?"

"Nanette Marx. Oh, you're teasing! Naughty girl. Listen, great news about your job! We'll have to have lunch and celebrate."

"What's there to celebrate? I'm only here behind a desk because I couldn't make a living as a writer."

"Isn't it awful? I tell you, the market's terrible. There are so many good writers around, talented writers like yourself, who just aren't selling. Look, Sharon, I've got something I'd like to send you. It's a really terrific story. It's about this woman whose husband has her arrested and sent to jail for conspiring with her lover to murder him. So she gets ten years. After she gets out he takes her back. The story begins on the day she comes back home. . . ."

"Thanks, Nanette, I think I'll be too busy to look at anything for a while. There is one manuscript I'd like you to send me, though."

"Sure, darling. What?"

"Mine."

My relations with Nanette never were cordial. Perhaps it was childish of me to hold a grudge, but I did. I also continued on the cool side with my editor in chief. He found it baffling initially, then frustrating, and finally infuriating. When he began to see that his days of ready access to my pants were over, he began to look for an excuse to fire me. He couldn't do it too flagrantly—not even as easily as he might have been able to purge another associate editor, since my arrival at Cartwright had been accompanied by certain trade winds of gossip. To toss me out too capriciously on my much whispered-about ass would have been to publicly confirm those rumors and worse yet, to advertise Cohen's loss of the sexual favors they celebrated.

My work was good. Not to put too fine a point on it, it was excellent. Editors gave increasing weight to my opinions and high marks to my editing. I made contact with a number of good agents around town and gradually began to ferret out book projects of my own.

My first important project came to me through an agent named Irwin Ross. He was a smooth-talking dapper little man who had recently left William Morris to set up shop on his own. I met him through Duncan Childs. Duncan had warned me about him.

"He's a good agent. He comes up with some interesting clients. But he's tough. He's a barracuda. You've got to watch out for him."

When Ross took me to lunch at Chez Raymond he was charm itself. Not long after that he sent over a manuscript for me to read. It was a book called *By the*

157

Throat by Jackson Mustafa Habib. It was a raw, frightening account of ghetto and prison life.

> *They told me, be cool or you be nothin. On the street, you learn that first. You lose your cool you lose control, man. The junkies noddin out and shittin they pants in the doorways, man, they losin they cool.*
>
> *Everybody gotta be cool. But the coolest was the players. The pimps. They be the ones drivin the bad rainbow-color Cadillacs, the Lincolns, wearin the cashmere threads. And they none of them ever made a false move.*
>
> *So I made up my mind to be a player. I be thirteen then, but a big kid. I got to walk like a player, talk like a player. I didn't have no bread to dress like no player, but I put some together with the change I rolled off the junkies. I knowed my mama didn't like how I was actin, but I didn't care. All I cared about was bein cool.*
>
> *Then I found out my mama was a ho.*
>
> *I felt bad, man. I felt so bad I didn't want to be cool no more. I just wanted to cry.*
>
> *But I wouldn't do it. If you gone be cool, you be cool. So I tole my mama I was gonna be her pimp.*
>
> *Mama like to go throo the roof. Tole me she was gone whup me upside the head if she ever hear me say anythin like that again. I was twice her size, but she could scare me. But I couldn't back down, you know, and be cool. So I started hustlin' my mama. I sweet-talked her, and I riffed on what made her feel good. I didn't let her play with my Johnson, like I did my sister. But I kept lettin her know I was the Man.*
>
> *But sugar, she say, I got me a man.*
>
> *Who is this dude? I ask her.*

They call him Sweet Willie.

Well I knowed who Sweet Willie was. Everybody knowed him. He was one baaad motherfucker. If I was gonna beat Sweet Willie out, I was gonna hafta be badder than him.

I was bigger than him. Thirteen years old, I was six foot two and two-twenty. But I had to be better, too. So I waited up for a year, workin out and practisin. All that time my mama's layin on her back or givin head in parked cars, and Sweet Willie's pocketin the long green.

Then I faced him down. Sweet Willie, I tole him, you keep away from Nellie Rae Washington, she my ho now.

Sweet Willie, he laff. Then he come at me with a razor.

I played it cool. I hit him in the eyes with a fistful of dry bleach I got in my pocket. I give him a knee in the balls. Then I slice that motherfucker with his own blade.

After that I run my mother, and my sister too. No problem from Sweet Willie. He sit on the streetcorner with his dark glasses an his hand out, and sometimes I drop a few bucks in it when I go by. We get along okay.

After the first few pages I was ready to throw it away. But something kept me at it and by the time I had gone through fifty pages I didn't know what to think. It might be the sleaziest garbage I had ever read, or it might be brilliant.

I wrestled with it for weeks. I was terrified by the violence of what went on in those pages, but I was fascinated as well. I began to think that if certain major cuts were made, if a couple of passages toward the end were put up front to clarify the motivation, if a lot of heavy rewriting were done to put it into a cogent, readable form. . . .

Meanwhile Irwin Ross had been on the telephone daily, pushing me for an answer.

"If you want my answer today, Irwin," I would tell him, "then the answer is no. If you want to wait and give me some time with this thing, maybe I can pull something out of it."

And so he would call me back the next day.

"Mustafa's anxious to know your reaction, Sharon. Eighteen years in the slammer has made him edgy."

"That's your problem, Irwin. This isn't something I can make my mind up on overnight. If you want the manuscript back right now, tell me. I'll get a messenger."

"Hey, take it easy. Nobody said anything about wanting it back. But maybe you'd like me to have Mustafa call you."

"God, no! I don't want that guy to have one idea in the world that someone named Sharon Clover even exists! I mean it, Irwin. The guy terrifies me. If I decide to buy the book, fine. But if I turn it down, I'd be looking for him around every corner coming after me with a meat cleaver!"

"Mustafa? He's a sweetheart. Wouldn't hurt a fly."

"What were those eighteen years up at Attica all about? Long visiting hours?"

By the Throat was billed as a novel. But if one quarter of what Jackson Mustafa Habib described was based on first-person experience, the man was in a class with Idi Amin as a first-rate blood-curdling experience.

Finally I managed to reduce to written instructions all the changes I thought the book needed in order to have a chance. It was a lot of work and I very much doubted that Jackson Mustafa Habib would be willing to do it. But I thought I had an obligation to lay it out for him. If the work was done, and done right, it could be a hell of a book.

I sent the manuscript back to Ross with a note attached.

Irwin: Here's what I think needs to be done with the book. Frankly, right now it's a mess. But there is something very compelling about the story and there are places where the imagery and description are extraordinarily arresting. The dialogue is another matter, but I wouldn't fool around with that. So now it's up to the wild man and to you. Let me know. Sharon.

A week later, at three o'clock on a Thursday afternoon, I heard a commotion out by the reception desk.

"Well, where the motherfuckin' hell *is* she?"

"I'm sorry, sir, but you can't go back there!"

"I can't do what? You jus' watch my ass!"

"Sir! No! I'll have to call the police!"

"Yeah? You do an' I'll squash yo' tits through that motherfuckin' typewriter, bitch!"

"Mr. Habib?" I said.

A black mountain swung around to face me. He was over six and a half feet tall and couldn't have weighed less than two hundred and eighty pounds. His head was shaved and the black dome gleamed in the fluorescent lighting. His nose was flattened and spread across most of his face. There was a dark scar that extended from the inner corner of his eyebrow to the left nostril. A full beard was twisted in a bristling scowl. When he saw me the scowl evaporated, and something like a gentle smile came on his face.

"Miss Clover?"

"Yes."

"Jackson Mustafa Habib." He extended a hand the size of my old shortstop's mitt. "Sorry about the ruckus. Just thought I might stop by and see you."

Claudia at the desk was poised, white-faced, with her hand on the telephone. I shook my head at her. "It's okay, Claudia. I'll talk to Mr. Habib in my office."

"Sorry to barge in like this, Miss Clover," he apologized as we walked down the carpeted corridor to my little office. "I got kind of up tight when Ross sent me back my book with yo' note onto it."

"He sent you my note? Wasn't that thoughtful of him."

We reached my office. It occurred to me that I was crazy to let myself be cooped up with this man in that tiny space, but I didn't want him running around loose. I was furious at Irwin Ross for this little maneuver. But now the damage was done.

"What can I do for you, Mr. Habib?" I asked in a voice that I hoped was not shaking as much on the outside as it was within.

"Well, to begin with, you can tell me what the fuck you mean by all them 'change thises' and 'tighten thats.' You'll excuse my language I hope, ma'am. I ain't spent much time in decent company the last eighteen years. You might find me a little rough."

"I . . . I'm afraid I can't help you. I don't have your manuscript here. I sent it back to Mr. Ross. Now, if you'd like, I'll write you. . . ."

162

"No problem. I got it here." He reached into a woven, brightly colored bag that he had slung around his shoulders, and pulled out his eight hundred page manuscript as if it were a magazine. He slapped it down onto my desk. "Okay, let's talk."

For the next several hours we labored over the manuscript. At times Mustafa would become incensed and leap up from his chair, and I was afraid he was going to explode and go on a reign of terror through the offices of Cartwright & Co., beginning with me. But each time he managed to get a grip on his temper. After awhile a grudging approval of what I was trying to do with his book began to emerge.

From time to time Duncan Childs stuck his head in the office to ask me something and I knew he was really checking to make sure I was all right. But by the time the end of the day came around, I was so engrossed in the way Mustafa's book was taking shape that I barely noticed Duncan.

"Six o'clock, Sharon. You about ready to knock off?"

"No, not yet."

"I can hang around a bit longer if you want me to walk you down."

"You go ahead. I'll see you tomorrow."

"All right." I had a vague sense that he lingered uneasily for a bit more, and then he was gone.

The next thing I knew the cleaning woman was making her rounds. And then after that it was quiet and I suddenly realized that it was nine o'clock at night and I was alone in the office with this eighteen-year veteran of Attica prison.

But I wasn't frightened anymore. I had learned a

great deal about Jackson Mustafa Habib in the hours we had spent together that afternoon. He had in him an enormous reservoir of violence, but it was by no means an uncontrolled violence. It was something that he used to achieve certain ends. But there was also an extraordinary gentleness about him, the gentleness that is characteristic of so many big men. Men whose very size inspires trepidation in smaller mortals often develop a basic sweetness. They do not need to be tough to get what they want.

Mustafa was not of the classic mold of this sort of man. He did use terror tactics when he thought they would serve a purpose. But for some reason he seemed to respect me, or perhaps he took pity on me. In any case, he stopped trumpeting and howling and beating his chest after awhile and worked diligently on the manuscript. He took my suggestions with much better grace than many other writers I've known. As we worked, the general structure of a very exciting book began to emerge.

Still, when it got to be nine o'clock I thought it was time to knock off for the night.

"Let's keep goin' awhile more," he said. "I'd sho' like to finish this now."

"Finish? We could be here all night!"

"No, ma'am!" He hit the desktop in his frustration, scattering papers and sending my telephone catapulting to the floor. He picked it up apologetically, his momentary display of violence replaced with an almost pleading earnestness. "I'm gettin' it much faster now. I get the idea of what you're sayin' to me. If we could just go over this last section here, I tell you, we could be done in an hour."

I sighed and looked skeptically at the two hundred page section he was talking about.

"Please?" I think he was afraid that if we stopped I would never take the time again to work with him.

"All right. Another hour. But I've got to get home sometime. And I don't like to wander around alone too late at night."

"I'll see you home safe. Nobody gone bother you none with me around."

I had to smile. "No, I don't suppose they are."

It was nearly eleven when we finished. I was tired and very hungry. There was still one more point, though, that had to be covered. I had avoided mentioning it out of embarrassment. But I knew it would come up in the editorial meeting and I knew it would be unprofessional of me to let it slide.

"Mustafa, I don't know how to say this, but . . ."

"What is it, Miss Clover?"

"It's . . . oh, God. . . ."

He looked worried. "Hey, I can fix anything. You just tell me what to do. Man, I want this book *bad*! You tell me what you don't like, I'll trash it or whatever you want."

I could feel the familiar telltale redhead flush steeping my cheeks a deep crimson. Maybe I shouldn't have even brought this up. After all, the guy *was* huge. . . .

"It's just . . . well, you have a tendency to exaggerate. Sometimes it's effective and sometimes it's counterproductive."

"Exaggerate?" He bristled. Even a slight ripple of displeasure from Jackson Mustafa Habib was enough to send waves of fear through me. "What you talkin' 'bout, exaggerate?"

I was in for it now. But I couldn't back down. "Mustafa," I said. "Mr. Habib, I'm sorry, but *nobody* has sixteen inches. That's just too much. The reader won't believe it and then it just casts a shadow of lack of credibility over the rest of that scene."

I couldn't look at him. I kept my eyes fixed on the page until the letters swam like inane newts across the white paper. My cheeks were burning and my skin was numb.

For a long time he didn't say anything. I think that he was as embarrassed as I was. Finally I forced myself to look up at him.

He was sitting quietly, slumped in his chair, twisting a ring on his finger. He smiled a little sheepishly and shrugged. His eyes stayed on the ring he was twisting. I felt terrible. I had caught him in an overstatement that went straight to the heart of his masculine ego.

"It be true, Miss Clover," he said.

"What?"

"It ain't no exaggeration."

"Are you saying. . . ?"

"Want I should show you?"

"No!"

Sixteen inches? Could it really be true? If it was, this was certainly the only time in my life I would ever get a chance to see anything so awesome.

How could I pass up an opportunity like that? It would be like being in Gizeh and not having a look at the Great Pyramid.

"Yes," I said.

Mustafa stood up, unbuckled his belt and undid the

button at the top of his pants. I sat back in my chair behind my desk, trying to adopt an editorial posture. He paused with his hand on his zipper, looking at me. I nodded. My throat was too dry to speak.

His zipper slid down its long track and the fly of his trousers fell open. I sat forward. He let his pants slide down.

Hanging from the base of his abdomen was the most extraordinary single human feature I have ever seen. Thick as a young tree, silky black and smooth, and in its dormant state fully as long as my forearm. My eyes widened like a child's in front of her first Christmas tree.

With a gesture that was half-casual, half-prideful, he lifted it from beneath with a finger and draped it over the edge of my desk.

"There it is. You understand, that ain't the full size."

"I understand."

"I could show you the full size, if you want."

I nodded.

"You want to?"

"Yes."

The embarrassment that filled the room like smoke a few minutes before had evaporated. He was in control of the situation now, a proud man who knew that he had something truly exceptional to offer. And I recognized that I was in the presence of greatness.

"You'll have to help."

"All right," I said quietly. I reached out and touched it with my fingers. I felt its soft, vital warmth, its rubbery surface, the silken promise of power. I squeezed it gently and closed my hand around it as far as it would go.

167

"Get naked."

I had no thought of arguing. In the presence of that naked monolith, it was nonsensical to be clothed. I stood up, took off my jacket, and laid it neatly on the chair. My eyes were on his eyes now as I unbuttoned my white linen blouse and pulled it loose from my skirt. There was no leering in his eyes, no anxious lust; just an overpowering sense of sexual sureness and control.

I shrugged the blouse off my shoulders and let it drop onto my jacket. I let my glance dart to the instrument that lay waiting on my desktop. It seemed to me that it had grown larger. I ran my hands up my sides and kneaded my naked breasts, feeling warmth and excitement flow into them. Mustafa's eyes burned. His penis stirred on the surface of the desk between us, a snake stretching in the sun.

I undid my belt and loosened my skirt. I let my hand slide down across my belly, massaging away the tightness and the constriction of the clothing. My pores were tingling with a sensual sharpness. I gripped my pubic mound to control the trembling that had begun in my hand and felt the rich moisture of desire that was seeping through the tight red curls.

Mustafa waited with controlled dignity. There was no change in his posture. No words of impatience came from his bearded lips. Only the gradual lengthening of his mighty penis gave any indication of what forces be at work inside him as I slowly shed my clothing.

I slid down my skirt and kicked it away with a small movement of my foot and ankle, vaguely aware of a deterioration in neatness with each garment I had taken off. All that remained now were my panties and a pair of soft moroccan leather boots. Mustafa's cock had traversed half the desk.

"It's magnificent," I admired.

"That ain't all of it yet."

I was fascinated by the degree of control he seemed to be able to exercise over this phenomenal appendage. Most men I had been with sprang to erection abruptly or else struggled desperately to produce a condition capable of piercing and entering a woman's body. Never before had I seen a man with such mastery of his sex that he could allow it to grow in stately orchestration, swelling as a symphony swells toward a pitch of *fortissimo* perfection. I was audience and conductor, both.

I came around and stood by him.

"May I hold it?" I asked. "Can I . . . do things with it?"

He held it out to me. I took it in both hands. It was shockingly heavy, like a log of wood, but alive. I raised it and pressed its length against my stomach. It was still soft enough to bend, though it reached from my navel all the way up between my breasts and tucked against the eaves of my chin. I hugged it against me, pressing down upon its dark head with the underside of my jaw.

"You ain't afraid," Mustafa noted.

"No."

"Most chicks be scared of it. The white ones especially."

"No," I said. "I'm not afraid." I had no idea what I would do with that fantastic organ. There was no way I could possibly fit one quarter of it inside me. If he were to enter me and thrust it home, he would split me in two as easily as a woodchopper cutting kindling. But I wasn't afraid of Mustafa. I trusted that gentleness that I had discerned in him during the course of the afternoon. I knew that he wouldn't hurt me. He knew the awful power of his majestic phallus.

I took off my panties and bent to remove my boots. As I bent over he caught hold of my open crotch with one of his big hands, his thumb filling the crease of my ass, his palm against my vulva, his fingers splayed out past my hill of hair and up across my belly.

"Leave the boots," he told me. "They look good."

I stayed bent over, moving lightly against his hand. After a moment I stood up. My back was to Mustafa. I stepped back against him, feeling his cock tucked downward along the tight vertical cleft of my buttocks. I reached between my legs and took hold of it, drawing it through.

"Lift me up."

He lowered himself behind me until the root of his cock was level with my crotch. I slid backward on it so that I was nestled firmly at its base. Then he straightened his legs, raising me up.

It was like sitting astride a wild black stallion. I clutched at the neck of the great beast as my legs dangled free above the floor. It shivered and bucked against my naked loins with a thrilling nervous energy. My whole weight bore me down against that living pole that separated my thighs and quivered against the tenderest parts of me.

"It's like a wild thing!" I exclaimed. "Does this hurt you? Can it hold me?"

"Don't you worry."

I pulled it tighter against me and felt myself slipping on it as my pussy dissolved with wetness. The overwhelming maleness of him suddenly crashed over me with the force of an ocean wave, and unexpectedly I felt an orgasm begin to swirl up through me.

But he wouldn't let me have it yet. He lifted me off him. My body was like a paper doll in his hands. He laid me out across my desk, on top of the piles of paper that were the book he had written in prison and that I'd spent weeks trying to solve.

The desire was still tearing at me. It was goading me to a kind of madness.

"Give it to me please," I said. I didn't really know what I was saying. The words were inadequate sleeves around a desperate inexpressible hunger. "Fuck me, oh God, make me come!"

"Easy." Mustafa brushed his bearded face up between my thighs and over my belly. His lips enveloped my breasts and his rough tongue scraped my nipples. His cock lay trembling above my front and I grabbed it with both hands and began to masturbate it. A vagrant thought crossed my mind that the issue had been settled, there was no question that sixteen inches was not an exaggeration, I could stop now.

But I couldn't stop. I was quite literally mad with desire. I raised my legs, pulling my knees up toward my chest to lift my clit so that it pressed against him. For a few minutes he let me rub. I began to feel the momentum again and strained toward the blissful release that was just a few hard strokes away. And again, just at the crucial moment, he withdrew.

"Oh, goddamn you!" I screamed, hitting my fists against his chest and crying with frustrated rage and desire. "I can't stand it! I want to come! I don't care if you kill me, just fuck me!" Tears were streaming down my cheeks, drenching them as the cheeks below were drenched with a sweeter liquid.

He lifted me again in his hands and pressed my belly to his mouth. I had no weight at all for him. He handled me as someone might handle a sandwich, turning me over in his grasp, pressing his lips and teeth against whatever part of me he chose. He nibbled at my thigh, sucked my pussy, nipped my ass and licked at the aching sensitivity of its tiny opening, moved his mouth with little clicking and sucking sounds up past my stomach to envelop each of my tits in turn.

Then he lowered me horizontally until the small of my back rested on his mammoth sexual spear. He held me easily in his hands at arm's length, like a baby. He looked down at me with half-lidded eyes and a faint smile hidden behind his beard. One hand was cradled beneath my head and neck, the other enclosed my crotch. I lay as he held me, not moving. Gradually I began to relax. The tidal wave of frenzy receded and something like calm settled over my limbs and into the depths of my womb. Something like calm, but it wasn't quite calm either.

Mustafa sat down on the floor, stretched himself out, and laid me down beside him. I took the head of his enormous erection between my hands like a chalice and brought it to my lips. I dotted it with small kisses. Then I brought my tongue into play, sponging the tip with moisture.

At last I brought it down to rest between my thighs. The hunger that stirred me now wasn't the turbulent surface storm that had raged earlier, but a hot wind in a cave somewhere far below the surface. Mustafa lay still. I spread myself wide and eased his turgid sex up against my opening. The lubricious walls of my cunt stretched to accommodate it. Slowly, slowly I took it in until my insides were filled to bursting, then I began to move upon it. Only the head fit inside me.

Mustafa lay still. He watched me and held himself with a mystic control. He let me govern the pace and the motion, and after a little while it started, the orgasmic prelude that earlier had whipped me into a frenzy. Now it came on with gentle whisperings at first, a soft breath that rustled my pores and nerve endings. Gradually it began to build, and I rode Mustafa's great steed at a faster gait. Soon we were at a gallop, the wind whipping my head in an ecstatic gale, and I was sobbing and laughing and I came.

He told me afterward that he could only do it that way, lying still while the woman moved upon him.

"If I tried to fuck you the way a normal man fucks you, I'd kill you."

"I know." I trembled. "But you didn't. I knew you wouldn't hurt me."

We dressed and left my office. The offices of Cartwright & Co. were deserted, dim with the single light from the reception area still burning. I locked up and we walked to the night elevator.

"Did you ever . . . hurt a woman?"

"Fuckin'?"

"Yes."

"No. This thing of mine got big when I was just a little kid, even before the rest of me got so big. I got a big sister, six years older than me. She used to like to play with it. When I was ten she saw it one time and she got me in her room and made me let her suck it.

After that she'd bring her girlfriends home from school and let them play with me."

"That's all in your book. It's all true, then?"

"All true. I got used to the fact that I couldn't fuck like regular folks do, slammin' all the way in. My sister Rosamund explained it to me. She showed me how to fuck her and her friends. They'd hold me down and one of them'd hold my cock, while the one who was gettin' it would fuck it till she got off."

We rode down in the night elevator. I signed us out of the building. We walked out through the postmidnight quiet of Lexington Avenue.

"I'll get a cab," I said.

"You want I should go with you?"

"No, that's okay, just put me in a cab."

We stared uptown, looking for a taxi light.

"I killed a man one time though, that way. In prison."

"What?"

"Yeah. A fink. He was stoolin' to the guards."

"You. . . ."

"Yeah. I buggered him. Split the little fucker right in two."

A cruising taxi swerved in front of a panel truck and screeched to a stop in front of us. Jackson Mustafa Habib opened the door for me.

"I'll work on this stuff," he said.

I got in. "Put that scene in the book," I said to him as I closed the door, then changed my mind. "No, don't!" I called through the window as the cab pulled out.

Gentle and considerate as he had been with me, my stretched pussy still ached so that it was uncomfortable for me to sit. It would be days before I could sit or walk normally, or make love again.

The taxi rattled south toward SoHo. I suffered agonies over every bump, holding myself up from the seat with my hand. When I thought about the little man who had died so horribly in Attica, I cringed.

Chapter 16

With the success of *By the Throat* I moved up into the full editor ranks. With the promotion went a nice raise. There was no reason for a young woman on the way up to keep on living in the miserable flat I had been inhabiting on Broome Street. Mandy was in town that spring and she helped me apartment hunt. I found a nice little place on West Seventy-fourth Street, just off Central Park West. It had a bedroom, a sunken living room and a kitchen about the size of a telephone booth. The view from the window was of a brick wall three feet away, but if you stuck your head out the window on a nice day and craned your neck sharply upward, you could catch a glimpse of a little slice of blue sky. That was all right. I wasn't home much in the daytime anyway. The view hardly mattered at night.

I didn't have much in the way of possessions to move. Mandy and I managed with the help of a borrowed station wagon and Len Cuyler, a dancer from her company whom she sometimes slept with. Liam begged off. He was hard at work on his book. There was an air of excitement among our crowd at the Lion's Head. The feeling was that this time he was really going to do it.

Joel Cohen insisted on taking me out for a drink after work on the day that my promotion took effect. I hadn't been with him socially, and certainly not sexually, since my tenure at Cartwright & Co. had begun a year and a half earlier. I felt that I had made my point. But a drink to celebrate a promotion was not strictly a social occasion. I didn't think it would confuse the boundaries I had laid down.

Joel saw things differently. We had a drink, and then another. I tried to leave, but he insisted on ordering another round.

"You haven't been good to me in a long time, Sharon," he said.

"What are you talking about, Joel? I brought in a hot book. I've been doing my job, haven't I?"

He shook his toad's head sorrowfully. "Oh, Sharon, Sharon. Don't you remember the great times we used to have? You didn't come out to the Hamptons once last summer. Molly's missed you. Everyone missed you." He took my hand. "I've missed you."

"Joel, I thought you understood how I felt about that. We have a professional relationship now. I think it would be too difficult to try to mix the two things. I love my work. I don't want to jeopardize it by becoming involved in a volatile romantic relationship."

"You could jeopardize it by *not* becoming involved," he said truculently.

178

"Joel, you don't mean that. Besides, I'm a good editor. You know I am. And a man like you has no trouble finding girls who're dying to have an affair—isn't that right?"

"Well . . . yes. Of course it is. But . . ."

"So it would be silly for us to become involved again. There are damn few good editors around, you've told me that yourself. As much as we might want the other thing, we've got to keep our priorities straight."

It took all my diplomatic skill to get rid of him without losing my job in the process. He wasn't fooled; Joel Cohen was many things, but he was not dimwitted. I had outmaneuvered him for the time being. But I knew that he would be waiting for me. I had made an enemy.

I met Mandy at the Paramount to see *The Firebrands,* Susan Carraway's new movie. It had just opened to rave reviews and there was a big crowd. We waited in line to see it and afterwards we walked uptown to my apartment for a late supper.

"Susan was fabulous," I said as I dexterously fried calves' liver and bacon in my little nook of a kitchen. "Have you seen much of her recently?"

"I saw her in L.A. last month. She asked about you."

"Did she?" I was pleased.

"You made a big impression on her." Mandy giggled, and so did I.

I dished the food onto plates and brought them to the table. Mandy had set it, complete with beautifully folded napkins and candlelight. In the center of the table was a bottle of Chateau Lafitte Rothschild and two

179

exquisite crystal wineglasses. It was my first dinner in my first decent apartment. My eyes misted over.

"Oh, Mandy . . . it's lovely!"

"You're the big time now, kid," she told me. She poured the glasses full of the rich red wine and handed one to me. "To the most beautiful and talented writer/editor in the Big Apple."

We touched glasses and drank.

After dinner we sat on the sofa and talked, listening to Brahms. It had been months since we'd made love, but tonight the mood was perfect. Soon we were kissing, long unhurried kisses, leaning back against the sofa. With each other we approached love differently than we did with a man—not just the difference in the sexual parts involved, but a difference in rhythm, a difference in understanding. Every touch was directed toward a particular sensation that didn't correspond to anything in a heterosexual coming together.

After awhile Mandy eased me down and began to undress me. I lay with eyes closed, feeling the warmth of the wine in me, letting the gentleness of the music and Mandy's gentle touch soothe and warm me. Cotton slid this way, silk slid that way, and I was naked. I smiled. With my eyes still closed, I could feel Mandy caressing and enjoying me with her eyes. There was the barely perceptible pressure of a fingertip against the inside of my knee and I let my thighs fall open to expose my petaled center to her view.

I didn't fall asleep, but drifted into an erotic trance. I could feel each pore of my body separately and each was a separate erogenous chip, sensitive to the still air, the gentle pulse of the symphony from the stereo speakers, the soft sensual presence of another woman's body.

When I opened my eyes Mandy was sitting nude at the other end of the sofa, smiling at me.

"My God, but you're beautiful," she said.

I opened my arms. She purred like a cat and stretched herself on top of me along the full length of my body. She hooked her feet inside my ankles and drew my legs farther apart, nestling the silken hill of her mound of Venus against mine. She rested on her elbows and sank her long fingers into my hair, massaging my scalp.

Her tongue snaked slowly out from between her closed lips and approached me, glistening pink. I sent mine out to meet it. The tips touched and played a moment. Then I reached up for her with my lips, taking the slick little spear of sensual flesh in them and sucking it down to me. Mandy didn't move it. She let it be drawn out as far as it would reach, and I sucked on it and moved my lips in and out on it until the tension began in her thighs and groin, and I felt the hot liquid flow from her pussy down onto mine. Then we hugged each other tight and kissed passionately. I reached down to caress her ass and slide my hand down between those smooth wonderful cheeks so unlike a man's, down the nearly hairless cleft to the cauldron of her cunt, and took her with my finger while she rubbed her clit against mine.

It wasn't a sudden climax, but the kind that can be recognized and savored from a long way away, like a home port seen from a ship at dawn on the horizon, but not reached until late in the day. We sailed through sparkling crystal waters to our destination, untroubled, confident in our vessel. When at last we touched shore, we clung to each other with pleasure and fell asleep wrapped in each other's arms.

There is a phrase in publishing jargon: "over the transom." In some ways it is not unlike what is meant in farm parlance when an animal is impregnated without benefit of proper family planning and it's said that the father "got over the fence." An "over the transom" manuscript is the bastard child of the publishing industry, not properly blessed by the union of editor and agent, but deposited by the mailman on the doorstep like a foundling. Generally such manuscripts are returned unread with a form note to the effect that "we regret that this material does not meet our current editorial needs."

I don't know what it was that made me take the time to read this one. It was not the first that I had ever received. The two or three previous submissions I had gotten in the mail I had glanced at, and had determined in half a dozen pages that the level of writing wasn't worth pursuing. When Nathaniel Bumpers' book came in I very nearly didn't look at it at all.

There was a note with it:

Dear Ms. Clover,

I am sending you my book because I had your name from a writer of my acquaintance, Otis James. Normally I would not pay a great deal of attention to a recommendation from Otis, but my ears perked up when he said that you turned down his book. That leads me to believe that you are most likely a woman of taste and judgment. I would be most happy if you would apply those qualities to this effort of mine.

Respectfully,
Nathaniel Bumpers

I remembered the book by Otis James. It had been sent to me through an agent. It was a piece of historical garbage about a gun-toting Jewish cowboy in nineteenth-century Japan. I had in fact turned it down. It was later picked up by another house and did badly.

I was amused by Bumpers' use of the James book as a negative reference. So instead of sending his manu-script back with the form letter or shipping it downstairs to the college graduate who now occupied my old office, I decided to take it home and read it.

It had never occurred to Asa that he would be rich, or famous, or anything other than exactly what he was. He had been happy enough in his little shack—had not thought of it as a shack, but as the place he lived. He knew perhaps that there was more to life, but he did not think he wanted it. He did not think it had anything to do with him.

He had carved stone since he was a boy. His father had put a chisel into his hands when he was six. He had never gone after the stone with a view of imposing a shape upon it. He felt a friendliness with the stone. It did not seem inanimate to him, but alive. Not just alive, but full of merriment and magic. The hammer and the chisel he wielded were the door knocker he tapped to ask—diffidently—for entry into the world of the stone.

183

*That people now were paying great prices for the
visions he escorted out of the granite blocks with his
carver's tools was a source of total bafflement to Asa.
But Julia understood it. Julia understood everything.
Julia told him not to worry about a thing. She told him
she would take care of him.*

So began the strange and wonderful story of a
backwoods stone carver who becomes the artistic mes-
siah of his age and the driven woman who engineers his
rise and fall. It had everything an editor dreams about:
an absorbing story, depth of feeling, unforgettable characters, insights, true significance. I was tired when I
got home and intended to read only a chapter or two to
put me to sleep. But when my clock radio went off at
seven in the morning I was still reading and I didn't put
the book down until I finished. And when I finished it I
wasn't tired anymore.

Chapter 17

Cohen disliked the book. I had sent it to him with a rhapsodic note attached. When I saw him in the hallway outside the conference room before our next editorial meeting he greeted me sarcastically.

"Who's the new boyfriend, Sharon?"

"What?"

"Whatsisname . . . Napoleon Bonaparte. The one who diddled that ecstasy out of you about the stonecutter book. I trust he's better in the sack than he is at the typewriter?"

"Are you talking about *Man of Stone*? The Nathaniel Bumpers book?"

"That sounds like it."

"I can't believe you don't like it."

For the next hour Joel Cohen tried his acid test to make a believer of me. He slashed me to ribbons with irony and barbs throughout the conference. The force of his rhetoric was such that I knew it would be pointless to circulate the book around to the other senior editors. There were none of them who would be willing to stand up to Cohen against that kind of disapproval.

I knew what the problem was. I made a severe tactical error by coming in with such enthusiasm on the property. I ought to have been cool about it, and perhaps conned Joel Cohen into thinking it was his discovery as much as mine. Joel had been looking for a way to cut me down to size. Here, with a book that I so obviously loved, he saw his chance

It made me furious. It was one thing to nurse a grudge against me for not sleeping with him anymore. But it was another thing altogether if he was going to let this vendetta obscure his professional judgment.

"All right, perhaps it needs a little polishing here and there, Joel. But this is a find!"

"I can't see it," he said smugly. "Listen, have your friend try again if you like. Maybe if you two cuddle together on it you can make something out of it. But I doubt it. Frankly, I'm surprised, Sharon. I thought you had a better head on your shoulders. I hate to see you start letting your libido rule your judgment."

I didn't slap him. I was going to do everything I could to overcome this petty personal jealousy. The book was too good to throw overboard. I spent two weeks going over it from every angle I could think of, drawing up pages of notes. I sent them to Mr. Bumpers along with his manuscript. I told him I couldn't promise anything, but if he made the changes I had suggested, I would do all I could to see that his book was accepted by Cartwright & Co.

* * *

Liam called me.

"Let's go out to dinner," he said.

"You sound chipper. What's the occasion?"

"No occasion. I just feel like taking my girl out to dinner. Do I need an occasion?"

He didn't need an occasion, but it certainly had been a fairly occasional practice. Still, I wanted to see him. We hadn't been very close during the past few months. Our relationship seemed to be on some strange tidal flow, with long ebbs when the tide stayed out and left me flopping like a beached fish on a sandbar. Then suddenly it would be high tide again and there would be Liam, full of charm, in thrall to whichever literary beacon he was following at the time. He was never predictable and never boring.

He arrived to pick me up at my apartment with a bouquet of roses. He looked splendid in a dazzling white suit. My guess was Tom Wolfe. It was a warm spring evening and I had put on an off-the-shoulder peasant blouse that revealed a provocative swell of bosom, and a full blue cotton skirt.

We took a taxi downtown. Liam was in high spirits. We went to a new restaurant on Bleecker Street that had recently been written up in all the magazines and was very current. It was an attractive place, with nostalgic lighting and lots of softly gleaming brass and mirrors. The hostess, a tall beautiful blonde, greeted us and showed us to our reserved table. I saw the way she looked at Liam and was reminded again of what a fabulously attractive man he was. It felt good to be with him.

"She likes you," I said. The hostess was moving among the tables, leaning over to ask people how they were enjoying their dinner. Her ass was eloquent against the soft drapery of her skirt.

"Oh? I didn't notice."

"The hell you didn't. Butter wouldn't melt in your mouth, would it?" I scooped up a pat of butter with my knife. "Here, put this in your mouth. Let's approach this scientifically."

"Science, that's the great thing these days. I was reading an item in the *Times* about research on the praying mantis. Fascinating stuff. Material for a whole novel there."

"They're the females who eat the males, right?"

"Correct. A form of life with an extremely limited sense of how to have a good time. Anyway, in this article, they told about these two researchers from the Smithsonian Tropical Research Institution in Panama who were studying the sex habits of the praying mantis."

"Under a federal grant, no doubt."

"Don't be small-minded, Sharon. These things are important. They have implications far beyond the narrow world of the praying mantis."

"Sorry."

"Anyway, their research was stymied by the fact that they couldn't get the goddamn praying mantises to fuck."

"I guess the males would have to be pretty horny, considering the consequences."

"They left them together during the daytime, but the damned insects just wouldn't do it. They tried everything—soft music, pornographic movies, candlelight. Nothing worked. And they didn't dare leave them together in the cage at night, because they knew the ladies would kill the males if they came groping after them in the dark. Praying mantises aren't big on fore-play. The only way the poor guy's got a chance is to sneak up and pounce.''

"But they wouldn't do it in the daylight?"

"No. Who can blame them? Have you ever taken a good look at a female praying mantis in broad daylight?"

"No."

"Pretty grisly. The Bo Derek of praying mantises is maybe a 'two.' Anyway, these researchers were going crazy. Here their federal grant is about to run out, and they couldn't get any hanky panky going with these weird insects. One night they couldn't sleep. They came into the lab just before dawn and discovered that the males were in their cage, hopping around panting and jerking off. This was the breakthrough they'd been looking for! It turned out that mating between praying mantises naturally occurs only in the last few minutes before sunrise, when there's just enough light for the poor guy to sneak up on his girlfriend and not enough to see how ugly she is.''

"This was all in the *Times*?"

"Most of it. I embellished a little. The researchers used the phrase 'a final libidinous leap' to describe the predawn kamikaze attack. I liked that."

I laughed. "Well, I promise not to kill you unless you don't leap."

It was one of the best times we'd ever spent to-gether. I was sure that there was something on Liam's mind and for the first part of the evening I kept waiting for him to bring it up. But he just went on spinning anecdotes and trading quips, and after awhile I was enjoying myself so much I didn't think about it anymore. After dinner we came uptown to The Red Parrot, where we danced and listened to Chris Connor. Around two in the morning we went back to my apartment and went to bed. We made slow, wonderful love. Liam was a sexual magician when he wanted to be and he was in top form that night. After many orgasms I finally drifted off to sleep with my hand locked around his penis.

But penises are changeable things. When I woke up in the morning Liam was gone. On the pillow where his head had been there was a rose, taken from the bouquet he had brought me the evening before.

Chapter 18

On Monday morning there was a cardboard carton on my desk when I arrived at the office. It was tied up with cotton twine. It had once contained Hellman's Imitation Mayonnaise.

Now it contained *Shadows of One Another*, by Liam McCorley.

I sat for a long time staring at the box. I didn't want to open it. I started sweating. It was difficult to breathe. I couldn't open a window; the windows didn't open. I got up and went out to the water cooler, then kept on walking and went downstairs and walked around the block.

When I came back it was still there. I knew I was having an hysterical reaction. But I also knew that somewhere in the back of my mind I had been expecting this moment ever since I had taken the job. And I had been dreading it.

How could I judge Liam's work? Should I not disqualify myself, like a judge who discerns a conflict of interest in a case? I could give it to Duncan to read. But that would be ducking the issue. Liam had brought it to me. He wamted me to read it. He wanted me to buy it. One way or another, I would have to give him an answer.

The coffee wagon came around. I went out and got a cup of strong black coffee. I came in and sat down again in front of the Hellman's Imitation Mayonnaise carton. I took my scissors and nipped the twine.

SHADOWS OF ONE ANOTHER
by Liam McCorley

Behold! human beings living in an underground den . . . Like ourselves . . . they see only their own shadows, or the shadows of one another, which the fire throws on the opposite wall of the cave.

Plato, The Republic

In my younger and more impressionable days in the great Middle West of this country, I was a chaser after rainbows and a dreamer of gossamer dreams. I might have been content to go on chasing and dreaming forever. But I came East to Princeton at the insistence of my father, who had trod that same path a quarter century earlier. There I joined the great idealistic swarm of unrest that was known as the anti-war movement, feckless youth with starry eyes and a vision of peace on earth. For a transitory enchanted moment we paid court to the last and greatest of all human dreams, the dream of brotherhood and peace on earth.

192

But when we touched that dream it shattered, disappearing into brightly colored spray like a soap bubble. And for a while I had no cause, and no dreams, only the foul dust that floated in their wake . . .

Something about this made me uneasy. And yet it was not such bad writing. A little flowery perhaps, a little archaic in style. But the imagery was strong, there was a certain poetry. . . .

In the late spring of that year I took a house along with another Princeton man on the southern shore of Long Island. The community in which I settled was one distinguished by great wealth. Along the shoreline great palaces shimmered in the sunlight, shedding yachts and tawny-limbed heiresses into the bay. The house which I shared with my friend was not of that stripe. It was a modest, boxy little bungalow that attached to the formidable spread of sleekness with the sly unobtrusiveness of a barnacle clinging to the belly of a yacht . . .

I will skip over the next few pages of the manuscript and get to the part that really began to worry me. The narrator's friend has begun seeing a married woman, a southern belle who is married to a Vietnam veteran who owns the local hardware store.

He told me that he had met her once many years before at a dance at a country club. They had danced all evening, absorbed in each other, moving like amorous wraiths through the white moonlight that fell on the terrace. Her voice was husky with whispers, and her

193

silvered slippers glided over the blue flagstones with the lightness of enchantment as the orchestra played.

And there had come a moment, a breathless, airless moment of incomparable magic, when the stars had stirred in the dark sky and descended about their shoulders, and her perishable lips had inclined upward toward his own. He had paused, exalted and yet half-regretful, knowing that the moment her lips touched his an unalterable alchemy would take place, and he would no longer vibrate in perfect tune with God and His universe. . . .

I sat back in shock, remembering Liam as I had first met him that night at the Lion's Head in his pinstriped suit and high collar, ordering a "martini cocktail." Like a character out of *The Great Gatsby.* . . .

There was a sick feeling in my stomach as I took another chapter from the Hellman's Imitation Mayonnaise carton.

In the morning it was raining. I walked down along the beach to look at the clouds. The clouds were coming in from the sea. The sea was gray and choppy, and the clouds were coming in.

I took the train into the city and went to the office. After work I took a taxi and went to O'Neal's for a drink. The rain had stopped. It was a fine evening. I sat at a table on the sidewalk and watched it get dark. Horse-cabs went by, clippety clopping through the heavy traffic toward Central Park. Lights began to come on. The taxis drove by full of passengers, and there were people on the sidewalks frantically looking for taxis. A taxi stopped in front of my table, and Bill Madox got out.

"Hello, Mike," he said. *"Where've you been?"*

"I've got a place out on the island. I don't spend much time in town any more. Have a drink."

"Thanks, I will."

Bill sat down. The waiter came and I ordered him a pernod. I ordered another one for myself.

"Do you still get out to the racetrack much, Mike?"

"No."

"Why not? You used to get a big kick out of the horses."

"I don't know. Maybe it's the betting. What about you, Bill? How are you doing?"

"Not so well, Mike. Not so well."

"What's the problem?"

"Money, Mike. Money's the problem. I'm behind on my rent. The landlord's going to throw me out."

I took out my wallet and handed him a twenty.

"Would that do you any good, Bill?"

"Yes."

He put it in his pocket. I knew that it would be gone in trips to the two dollar window at Belmont long before his landlord had a chance to lay a hand on it.

"What have you been writing lately, Bill?"

"Not writing. Hadn't you heard? Nobody writes any more."

"No?"

"No. Thinking's the great thing now. That's what they're all doing. Thinking. Conceptual prose."

"What about the writing?"

"That's out. Writing ruins it. It's the thought that counts. Once you put it on paper, it's corrupted."

"Go on," I said. I ordered us a couple more pernods.

195

"The way it works," Bill explained, "is that you think great books. They stay in your head, and nobody else ever sees them. They never suffer from being crammed into little words and mangled through a typewriter."

"Outfoxes the critics, too, I bet."

"That's it, Mike. You've got the idea. Nullum criticum observandus est. Don't give the critics a peek. The watchword of a whole new literary generation."

"This is great stuff, Bill. Where does it come from?"

"Jonathan Richards thought it up. He's one of the new writers. It's a gesture of contempt to all the publishers who've turned down his books. Now they're begging for his stuff."

Two hansom cabs came down the street and pulled up in front of O'Neal's. A group of laughing young men piled out. They were slim-hipped and limp-wristed, and their hair was cut very short. They swept by our table and went inside. With them was Sylvia. She was wearing tight jeans and a very expensive sweater. And she was very much with them . . .

And so it went. After Hemingway there was a section in which he seemed to confuse Thomas Wolfe and Tom Wolfe:

Oh, the wonder, the vast windswept magic of the land! I lay upon the purple hillside, a prisoner of my timid soul, and listened to the distant mournful whistle—bwaaap! zannngg! chuggachuggachugga!—of a train that was bound I knew not whither and would not come again. O America! Zowie! I raised my eyes to the

196

distant horizon, and saw the first bright twinkling of a
star. . . .

A section in which he acquires a motorcycle with a
sidecar, picks up a transsexual rape victim who is hitch-
hiking with her pet bear, and takes a job teaching
wrestling in a private school, called to mind inevitable
comparisons with John Irving. Later he kills an old
pawnbroker, is racked by terrible guilt, and nearly winds
up confessing to the prosecutor. But at the last minute
he decides to take it on the lam.

The motorcycle was parked on the edge of the
concrete highway, its rear wheel sitting in the yellow
dust, amid patches of dry, matted grass, its front wheel
resting on the hot dark concrete that stretched out
straight and endless beneath the broiling sun. Rebecca
hunkered down in the dust, drawing in the dust with a
stick. Nearby her bear lay in the cool shade of the
drainage ditch, watching the endless busy movement of
the insects, the grasshoppers, the ants moving through
the scraggly grass carrying seeds and barley beards
back to a waiting anthill.

"So you're really goin', Mike?"

"Reckon so."

"Where'll you go?" She looked up at me anxious-
ly. "You ain't gonna get in no more trouble, are you,
Mike?"

"No. I'll be—I don't know. I ain't really figured it
out yet. But I'll be around. Maybe there's no one place
special anyone has to be. And then I'll be everywhere.
I'll be in the anti-nuke rallies, when the people lift up
their voice against the threat of global destruction. I'll

be in the Third World countries as they struggle against imperialist oppression. And I'll be in the way lovers look at each other when their bodies stir with passion and they want to make love . . ."

"You be careful now, Mike." A tear trembled in her eye, and I knew she was thinking of the gentle love I had made to her, and how I had brought her back from the terrible trauma of her rape.

"Sure. I will."

I climbed on the motorcycle, and kicked the starter. The engine roared to life. The bear rolled over and sat up in the grass, blinking, startled. I eased the bike out onto the highway. I looked back over my shoulder once to wave.

THE END

Chapter 19

As I feared, my relationship with Liam didn't survive my rejection of his novel. Perhaps "feared" isn't the right word. There must have been a part of me all along that had known it couldn't last; that hadn't wanted it to. Liam had been a god to me in those dewy-eyed days when I first dipped my oar, as it were, in New York's literary waters. But I had outgrown the days when I welcomed that kind of intellectual domination. And then, I think I had known for a long time without admitting it that Liam was a fraud.

I don't condemn him for it. There are a lot of writers like Liam. Some are more skilled in concealing the source of their inspiration, or at blending styles together to arrive at an unidentifiable homogeny. Even the best writers are influenced by somebody. But Liam seemed to be influenced by just about everybody.

I called him. It was agony, but I couldn't just send back the Hellman's box with a rejection letter.

"I can't accept it, Liam. I'm really sorry."

"What do you mean, you can't accept it?"

"It's just not . . . I don't know. . . ."

"It's just not what?" What don't you know?"

"Original enough."

There was a long pause. The telephone wires hummed with bated breath. "It's not?"

"No."

Then angry: "What the hell do you know? What makes you such a goddamn expert? Just because you spent a year in Paris, you think you're Gertrude Stein?"

The whole buckshot spray of it stung, but that last pellet in particular struck home. That lie about Paris had been made a long time ago. I had forgotten about it. But I had never taken it back. Who was I, indeed, to be making judgments about pretension, literary or otherwise?

Except that it was my job.

"I was never in Paris, Liam. When you met me I was straight off the bus from Minneapolis. I didn't know a thing about writing. You taught me a lot, and not just about writing. But darling, I can't buy your book."

"You've never been to Paris?"

"No."

"What about the Rue Madeleine? What about Shakespeare and Company? The Deux Magots?"

"All out of books," I admitted. "Books and movies."

This time there was a very long pause. Was he still there?

"Are you okay, Liam?"

"Sure. Listen, I'm going to be taking off for a while."

"Where will you go? What will you do?"

Unwittingly, I had given him the perfect cue.

"Frankly my dear," he intoned, "I don't give a damn."

We haven't seen each other since. But from time to time I hear news of Liam from mutual friends. He is living in Hollywood now, writing for the movies. Apparently he is doing very well.

Nathaniel Bumpers completed the revisions I had suggested to him and returned them to me.

They were brilliant.

What stray misgivings I may still have had about the book as a result of the disparagement of my editor in chief were put to rest. Bumpers was a writer of rare talent. And, I had to admit, I was no slouch as an editor, either. I had identified the few weaknesses in the original version and Bumpers had bettered them. He was complimentary in his cover letter to me.

> I might as well admit that I was a bit
> sore when I got your notes. I felt like a parent
> of a newborn babe whose pediatrician is
> recommending cosmetic surgery. *My* baby?
>
> I must say I enjoyed my righteous in-
> dignation. It was a bit of a comedown when I
> read *Man of Stone* over again and discovered
> you were right. Not just forgivable, but nail-

on-the-head, point-for-point right. If this book makes it, I'll owe you a lot.

> With appreciation,
> Nathaniel Bumpers

"No."

"Joel, you can't be serious."

"It was crap before and it's crap now. You'll never be an editor, Sharon, until you learn to put your personal life aside and deal with a book strictly on its merits."

"For God's sake, Joel, my personal life has nothing to do with this."

"So you say."

"Are you sure it's not you who's getting . . . ."

"Don't try to tell me my business," he snapped. "I think I still know a bit more than you about publishing."

"Then what is it, Joel? Is it me?"

For a moment a look of hurt and passion flickered on his face. Then it disappeared behind his superior mask.

"Do your job, Sharon," he said, "or you won't last very long around here."

I called an editor I knew at another house, told him I had a book for him then sent it over by messenger. Two days later he called me.

"Hi, Sharon, it's Ed. Hey, this book is pretty good!"

"You're damned right it's good. It's better than good."

"You're right. So what's the story? Why aren't you guys publishing it?"

"Byzantine reasons, Ed. You don't want to know. Are you going to make Bumpers an offer?"

"I sure am. What do you think he'll go for?"

"What are you planning to offer?"

"What do you think—fifteen?"

"Fifteen thousand? Ed, you better go back and reread that book. You're holding a book that's going to be a best seller *and* a critical smash. Money and prestige, Ed. Don't try to cut it too close."

"But, Sharon, a first novel . . ."

"So what? We're talking about what's on paper there, Ed. If you don't think you can sell that, that's fine. But if you're not prepared to make him a decent offer, give it back to me and I'll send it to another friend."

"No, now wait a minute, Sharon, I didn't say we wouldn't go any higher. I was just throwing that out. Let me get back to you."

Three phone calls later we had agreed on an offer of forty thousand in advance, with royalties scaled at ten, twelve and a half and fifteen percent.

I sent Bumpers a note explaining that internal difficulties at Cartwright had forced me to pass on his book, but that I had taken the liberty of sending it on to another publisher who was very excited about it. A week later I had this reply:

Dear Miss Clover,

Your friend certainly was excited. Damn, *I'm* excited! I didn't know people spent that kind of money on books, except maybe for books with names like *Passion's Purple Promise*.

Sharon

I am sorry it won't be you bringing *Man of Stone* into the world. You are one heck of a good editor. The book has profited greatly from your experience and wisdom.

Besides, I'll miss our correspondence. Maybe we can try again someday on another book. I'm not much of one for getting to New York, but if you're ever up this way I'd be pleased to buy you a cup of coffee.

Best regards,
Nathaniel Bumpers

Man of Stone was a sensation. Word was out on it long before it reached the stands. It was selected as a book club alternate. *Publishers Weekly* hailed the "staggering new talent." The *Times* reviewer wrote that "Mr. Bumpers has succeeded in effecting an extraordinary tandem: he has combined pulse-racing passion with an ethereal spirituality that produces one of the most original works of fiction in many years." *Newsweek* raved. *Time* sang.

Ed sent me over an advance copy. Paper-clipped to the jacket was a note on his memo paper that said: "Congratulations." I held the book in my hands, smelling its newness, admiring the clean simple cover that showed a dusty hammer and chisel between the title and the author's name.

I was curious to see what Nathaniel Bumpers looked like. But the picture on the back was a long shot of the author hunched over a typewriter on the porch of a cabin in the woods. There was no way of telling whether he was old or young, fat or slim, much less any clue to the particular look of his features.

Sharon

I opened the book to the title page. On the page opposite was the dedication.

To Sharon Clover

Oh boy, Sharon, I said to myself, are you in for it now.

Chapter 20

Joel Cohen was livid.

"Do you realize what you've done? You've let the book of the goddamn decade slip through your fingers!"

"Joel, you turned it down flat."

"Don't tell me what *I* did! It was your book. *You* let it go! And you've got your name right there on the dedication page. How did *that* happen, Sharon?"

"Joel, I swear I knew nothing about it until this morning."

"I was right," he said with bitter triumph. "You *were* fucking him. That was the whole problem in the first place."

"Damnit Joel, I have never met Nathaniel Bumpers in my life!"

"Don't give me that." He picked up the book from his desk. "To Sharon Clover. Jesus H. Christ! Won't that make a nice human interest story in the trade press!"

"Nobody cleared that with me. Obviously I . . ."

"Nobody cleared it, did they? Well *I'll* clear something with you. Clear out! Clear out your desk and clear out of here! Go to another publisher, go to New Hampshire, go to hell! You're fired!"

"That's clear enough. Just one thing, Joel."

"Yes? What's that?"

The slap was satisfying. My hand still stung from it as I went through my desk, emptying my personal effects into my briefcase. My secretary Joanna would go through the files later and forward anything that I might need. I was burning with the cold clear flame of righteous indignation. Fired? Nothing could suit me better than to get out of this place.

I snapped my briefcase shut. I left on my desk a pen and pencil set that had been a gift from Duncan Childs on my promotion to editor. It was a heavy mounted desk set and I decided to leave it for Joanna to pack. I thought about Duncan, off in Florence. He had gotten a bug about going to Italy. He had decided to go and try to become an editor there. After spending six months studying the language in the evenings at an institute, one day he just quit his job and took off.

"*Arrivederla, Sharonissima*," he had said to me with a cheery wave. "When you drink Campari—and you will—think of me."

That was back in November. I'd received a couple of postcards from him since. Duncan was still struggling to master Italian. He hadn't found work in publishing. He had found a job with an American company that exported handbags.

It's not very literary work (he wrote), but
I am in the city where Dante lived and wrote.
It is a beautiful place. And I keep looking for
my Beatrice on the bridge. I know what she
looks like. She has red hair.

I took a last look around my office. Thirty floors
below, Lexington Avenue swarmed with midday traffic. It was a wonderful view from up here. I wondered
how it was going to look from down there.

I didn't say good-bye to anybody. The last thing I
wanted was to get emotional and leave with mascara
streaking my cheeks. I was waiting for the elevator
when I saw Claudia, the receptionist, signaling to me
through the glass door. I had a phone call.

"It's Mr. Bumpers. Do you want to take it, or
shall I have him call back after lunch?"

"No, I'd better take it now."

I went back to my office and picked up the phone.

"Miss Clover? Nat Bumpers. Seems like I've made
it down to your neck of the woods after all. Can I buy
you that cup of coffee and some lunch to go along with
it? If you're free on this short notice."

"Mr. Bumpers, as it happens, you catch me at a
moment when I am exceptionally free, thanks to you."

"Well, I'm not sure what I had to do with it, but if
you're free for lunch, that's good enough for me. Shall
I pick you up at your office?"

"Better not. Where are you staying? I'll meet you
at your hotel."

He was staying at the Algonquin. We arranged to
meet in the bar. I walked over. It wasn't until I
was crossing Sixth Avenue that it occurred to me

that we had not established any signal for recognition.

But despite the unrevealing photograph on his dust jacket, I didn't think I would need a carnation in a buttonhole to know Nathaniel Bumpers. I had a strong visual image of the author of *Man of Stone*. A woodsman, with wide shoulders and big hands. He would be bearded and slightly balding, yellow hair beginning to fade to white. He must be about fifty-five. I was identifying him totally, I knew, with Asa Brooke, his protagonist in *Man of Stone*. It was Asa Brooke who was a real person for me, not his creator. To me the two men were the same creature.

I remembered the description of the young Asa.

He went at his work with a perfect golden concentration. The fluid sweep of his thick young arms was in no way separate from the thought behind his gentle eyes. Thought, yes; there was never more than one there at a time. Asa was not built for complexity. His genius was in his total absorption in the simple.

And later, when everything has fallen apart for him, and he is back again alone in the New Hampshire cabin where it had all begun (and which looked in the jacket photo exactly as I had pictured it when I read the book):

But the view was the same. The mountains, round-shouldered and peaceful, rose and fell in the same silhouette against the sky. The trees were taller and fuller near the cabin, but they were the same trees. And if those were not the same frogs croaking in the cool shadows of the quarry pool, they were surely close kin.

210

*And Asa felt the same close kinship with it all that
he had known as a young man. Closer, now. He was
round-shouldered with age like the mountains; not taller, but fuller, like the trees.*

*He lifted the stone and put it on the carving stand.
It was heavy and cool, and there was nothing more real.
There was a story inside it.*

This was the man I was looking for as I entered the
Algonquin. Round-shouldered, thick-waisted, with
gnarled workman's hands and gentle blue eyes.

I was right about the blue eyes. The rest was a
shock. The man whom I saw sitting at the bar sipping a
glass of beer and browsing through the newspaper was
about thirty. His blond hair was receding at the temples
and curled a little below his ears. He had a strong,
handsome face, a wide jaw and a small, almost feminine mouth. He wore round rimless glasses that looked
incongruous on him. He was wearing a tweed jacket
that he had probably had since college, a black wool
necktie and brown corduroy slacks. On his feet he wore
a pair of mud-streaked clodhoppers.

I looked around the place again to make sure there
was not a more likely candidate. There was not. The
other customers were businessmen and women, and a
couple of cartoonists comparing rejected drawings.

"Mr. Bumpers?"

He looked up with a shy smile. "Yes?" He looked
confused when he saw me. "Oh," he said, "you're
not . . ."

"I'm Sharon Clover."

His jaw quite literally dropped. "Holy Moses!
You're Sharon Clover?"

"That's me."

He shook his head. "Well, I never thought you'd be anything like this. I thought you'd be . . . older, perhaps."

I grinned. "I was looking for Asa Brooke."

"Asa?" He laughed, delighted, which made his face flush and his eyes sparkle behind the round granny glasses. "No, I'm not there yet. But how did you get to be so smart about editing and still stay so young?"

"Keep on like that and I'll forget I'm mad at you."

His face sobered immediately. "Mad? Oh no, I sure hope not. What about?"

"That dedication."

"But I dedicated it to you. I told you in my letter I owed the whole thing to you, the way it worked out. I just wanted to show you I really meant it. Gosh, if I did anything wrong, Miss Clover, I'm sorry as heck."

"You should have checked with me first. I was working for another publisher."

"I never thought about that. Damn, I'm sorry. I just thought that because you people had passed on it, there wouldn't be . . . I hope it hasn't caused you any trouble, Miss Clover."

"Nothing serious. I was fired just before you called."

"What?" He rose up off his stool. "They can't do that to you! Look, let me talk to them. I'll tell them it was all my doing. I'll tell them how much you put into the book, how. . . ."

I had to calm him down. He was terribly upset. All through lunch, which we had in the hotel restaurant, he kept apologizing and trying to come up with bigger and better ways of making it up to me. I assured him it wasn't necessary.

"I'm happy to be out of there, really."

"But you can get another editing job like that," he said, snapping his fingers to demonstrate the ease with which I could do it.

"I'm not sure I want one. It's a frustrating business. I'm always feeling caught between my responsibility to the author and to the publisher. Like a double agent."

His face lit up. "Hey, that's it! Why not be an agent? I'll be your first client!"

"Oh no, I don't think so."

"Well sure! Look, Ed told me what you did for me on that contract. You sold the book for me, you got me that big advance. If it hadn't been for you, who knows what would have happened? One of the reasons I had to come into New York is to interview agents. Ed says I've got to have one, with all the stuff that's happening now with *Man of Stone*. I'm supposed to meet this afternoon with some guy named William Morris, and Sterling Lloyd or something, and a couple of others. Look, if you'll take me on, I won't have to see any of those people. You can show me the sights instead."

"Really, it's out of the question. I can't just . . . become an agent. I don't know anything about it."

"You did a pretty good job for me. Ten percent of all this stuff I'm getting is rightfully yours. I'd sure as heck hate to see it go to anybody else."

I had arrived at one of those unexpected corners life surprises you with. Out of nowhere there it is and suddenly you're on a whole new street. I knew next to nothing about being an agent, but I knew I could learn. and Nathaniel Bumpers was a pretty good client to be starting out with.

"What sights would you like to see?" I asked him.

Chapter 21

Nat Bumpers had a car. It was a 1962 Jeep wagon that looked as if it never could have been new. But we did the town in it, and in spite of my secret conviction that it would disintegrate in the middle of the West Side Highway, we managed to get to the Cloisters, the Brooklyn Bridge, the Empire State Building and the Museum of Modern Art all in one afternoon. I was exhausted by the time we pulled up in front of my building on West Seventy-fourth.

"What shall we do tonight? How about a play?"

"A play?" The man was clearly insane, or bionic. "Haven't you done enough for one day?"

He laughed. "As long as we're in New York, might as well take advantage of it. I'll see what tickets I can get and pick you up in an hour." A look of concern crossed his face. "Unless you've already got plans."

"Plans? Me? No, I was just going to settle in with some alcohol and amphetamines for a good rest."

"Don't tell me you're tired!"

"I wasn't going to tell you. Fatigue ripped it out of me."

"I'm sorry. Maybe I go a little crazy in the big city. It's the first time I've been here in fourteen years. I've already taken too much advantage of your good nature. Can I call you tomorrow?"

"Sure. We'll have to work out this agent business. Listen, I really enjoyed this afternoon."

"You did? I sure did too."

As I was getting out of the car, a green Pontiac pulled out of the parking space just ahead. I stuck my head back in the window. "There's a parking space," I said, "if you'd like to come up for a drink."

We had a few drinks. We took off our shoes and put our feet up, relaxing and talking. The fatigue passed and a wonderful languor took hold of us. He told me about growing up in New England, and I told him about growing up in the Midwest. I told him about playing shortstop. He told me about taking cars apart and putting them back together. When he was eighteen he had hitchhiked to Alberta and had gotten a job on a cattle ranch for the summer. There had been an old paperback copy of Conrad's *Lord Jim* in the bunkhouse and he had read it. Up until then Nat had given little thought to what he wanted to do with his life. The book inspired him to become a writer.

It also had inspired him to become a seaman. He had journeyed out to the Pacific coast and signed on aboard a tramp steamer bound for the Orient. For the next six years he had sailed the world, keeping journals, writing stories. He had also taken up carving in the long weeks and months at sea. When he finally gave up the sailor's life he came back to Peterborough, New Hampshire, and built himself a cabin in the woods. For the last five years he had been there, making a living off odd jobs, getting his fulfillment out of life in carving wood and stone, and writing. He had made several false starts on *Man of Stone*. In the first drafts it had been a seafaring story. It was when he eliminated the nautical setting and chose the stonecutter theme around which to organize his story that it finally began to come together. That had been four years ago.

I lay on the sofa. Nat was in one armchair, his feet stretched out across the other. He seemed even more attractive than I had thought at first. With his jacket and tie off and his shirt unbuttoned to his chest, I could see that his body was densely muscled and hard. As he talked about his life, his features were reinforced in my mind with invisible accents, so that what had before been vaguely handsome now became a face rich in character and strength. He was a great writer, poised on the brink of what was surely going to be an extraordinary career. And he had invited me to share that career with him. It was an incredible opportunity. I was glad I had the sense not to turn it down. At the same time, I couldn't keep from wondering whether I would get a chance to share any more of his life.

"My God," I realized suddenly, "it's quarter past ten. You must be starved."

"Is it that late? I guess I ought to go."

"No, let me fix you something to eat first. Let's see what I've got."

We examined the contents of my larder and together

we assembled a strange and wonderful fish chowder. I had a full jug of soave on top of the refrigerator. We ate and drank and talked some more.

In the end, when I had pretty much given up hope of it, and had almost forgotten I wanted it, he kissed me. It began as a sort of shy good-night kiss. But then somehow we stepped through a looking glass that was made of tiredness and wine and confidences among virtual strangers, and we were in another world.

He lifted me in his arms and carried me into the bedroom. It was an exotic feeling, to be carried to bed—like a movie romance, like Gable and Leigh. His lips did not leave mine and my tongue explored the inside of his mouth as he lowered me to the surface of the bed and stretched out beside me.

I began to come alive with desire. My breasts ached. The nipples had grown stiff and were tugging outward as if they wished to leave my body. I wanted to attack him, to tear off his clothes and fasten my lips to his penis. I wanted myself naked to his eyes and to his touch. I wanted him inside me.

But I was afraid of scaring him off. It would be better, I thought, if I let him set the pace. So we kissed and he stroked my hair. I pressed my buttocks against the bed to assuage the tingling heat that he had aroused between them.

"Sharon," he said. It wasn't a question, only a sounding of the name like a musical note. But I answered.

Then Nat's hands began to move over my body. He kissed the hollow of my throat and I locked my fingers in his fine yellow hair, drawing him tight against me. With each new discovery of his exploring hands I moaned. When he brought them up under my skirt and found the wet silk of my panties I whimpered with pleasure. I raised my hips and he pulled the panties down.

When a woman's panties have been removed, the rules of the encounter change. There is no barrier left on the field that carries any significance. With his action and my consent, we had declared our purpose fully, and I no longer felt constrained to wait upon his lead.

We stripped away the remaining clothing quickly. Nat's cock was a hard clean cylinder. I took it lightly in my fingers, feeling the vibration of passion that trembled from it. He leaned forward with a groan and crushed his mouth against my breast, devouring the nipple with his lips and tongue. Pleasure spread through me and I couldn't keep still. I put his erection against my belly and rubbed it there. I squeezed my thighs together and felt that my clit was floating in a sea of oil. His hand came down, separated my legs. Seeing how wet I had become excited him more. He slipped two fingers into me, rubbing my clit with his thumb. I spread my legs as wide as they would go, forcing more tension into my clit, and my hips jerked as I came against his hand.

"Oh, but you're good, Sharon," he murmured. He kneaded my ass and thighs with the rich juice of my coming. My orgasm was like a bowl beneath a faucet that begins to fill again as soon as it is spilled. I wanted him inside me now, and I moved so that my knees bracketed his muscle-sheathed rib cage. The furrow of my cunt pressed against the long shaft of his sex. The head, like a heat-seeking missile, leapt toward the opening and plunged deep inside me. I shivered with each exquisite stab, aware of every sensation—the taste of his lips and tongue, the sounds of our moaning and the wet slap of our loins coming together, the sharp sweet smell of our mingled sexes, and the pulsing drive of his cock that filled me.

After we came I fell asleep. I awoke at some later point in the night. His arm was around me, my head was on his chest. My hand was curled around his penis, which wasn't erect, but not quite soft either. The semi-erection aroused a feeling in me that was not the raging desire I had felt earlier, but a sort of sexual tenderness. I moved my head down over his belly until I could take the half-formed creature into my mouth. I licked it gently and massaged it with the soft insides of my cheek. It grew until it was rigid, but I kept my movements soothing and Nat didn't wake up. It was an extraordinary sense of intimacy, as if I were his dream.

And again later I half-awoke to feel Nat fondling me. We were cuddled spoon fashion now and he stroked my breasts as one might stroke the head of a sleeping child. I sighed contentedly and let myself stay in the floating current of sleep where I was. His cock grew hard against my ass, then very carefully he shifted so that he could insert it into me from behind without disturbing me. He slid it in easily up the lubricated channel, but he didn't begin to pump. He lay there, buried deep within me, and I felt his thick throbbing presence. Locked together in that way we fell asleep again.

I woke up in the morning hearing his voice. He was not in the bed with me.

"Nat?" I called.

". . . really a beautiful piece of work, Mr. Bump-

220

ers,'' another man's voice said near my ear. I snatched
the sheet up over me and spun around.

The television set was on. It was the *Today* show.
Nat was on the screen, being interviewed by Gene
Shalit. He had mentioned *Today*, but it had been early
in the afternoon when we were racing around town, and
I had completely forgotten. Nat had hooked the television up to the timer I kept by the lamp to confuse
burglars on weekends when I was away. It must have
just come on.

"And so you worked away for all those years up in
your little cabin in the pines. When it was finally done,
how did you go about getting the attention of the New
York publishing world?"

"Well, Mr. Shalit. . . .'' Here his eyes shifted
for a moment to the camera and I felt that he was
looking directly at me. ". . . I happen to have the best
agent in the business. Sharon Clover.''

Chapter 22

I became something unusual in the business of literary representation: an overnight sensation. It was my association with Nat Bumpers, plus his nationwide TV testimonial, that did it for me. Suddenly I was the hot agent, without the first idea of how to handle the job.

Fortunately, there were many people willing to help me learn. I received offers from several agencies. My instinct was not to get swallowed up in the tar pits of a mammoth institution, where I would be prey to the sort of jealousy and backstabbing that I know went on in such places. From my experience in the publishing end I knew that William Morris on the East Coast can have a hell of a time getting a straight answer from William Morris on the West Coast. This didn't seem the right environment for a sweet young thing learning the ropes while at the same time carrying the kind of clients that more seasoned agents would kill for.

Sharon

I decided to team up with Barbara Dannenberg, an agent with whom I had worked several times during my editorial tenure at Cartwright. Barbara was a tough, canny agent with a reputation for getting the most out of a deal. Her big, New York-accented voice left people who had known her only by telephone unprepared for the chic, diminutive lady they met in the flesh. She had a firm devotion to the philosophical principle that it is the squeaky wheel that gets the oil. She also was the most honest and dedicated agent I had dealt with. Editors who knew her respected her, and there were few who didn't know her. She cared about her clients and they seemed to care about her. That was the sort of agent I thought I'd like to be. Although I did not expect to become involved to the same degree with all my clients as I had with my first.

As for my involvement with Nat Bumpers, it seemed to have been knocked off line by that first night explosion. When he returned later that morning from the television studio, he had been as stiff and awkward as a boy at his first dance. He seemed to feel, in the light of day, that he had trespassed into forbidden territory. Our intimacy jarred against the boundaries of a relationship begun and slated to continue as a professional one. His reserve hurt me, but it was also contagious. Neither of us seemed to know how to behave. We tried to return to the friendly give-and-take that we had started on the previous day, but it didn't seem to be there anymore. Our lovemaking sat between us, a beautiful and tempting stranger we could not ignore, but were unwilling to invite into the conversation.

"I'll start sorting through those movie offers this week," I told him. "We should be able to narrow it

224

Sharon

down to a few serious possibilities pretty quickly and take the bidding from there.''

"I'll trust your judgment on that.''

"What's your position on the screenplay? Do you want to write it?''

"Gosh, I don't know. I'd hate to see it get messed up by somebody who didn't understand the book. But I don't know a thing about writing for the movies.''

"I'll get you script approval. They're not going to like it, but they'll have to live with it.''

We talked like that. We sat across the breakfast table with cups of coffee chaperoning our hands. When Nat left, we said good-bye at the door without even shaking hands. He grinned shyly and gave a sort of a wave. I stood there a half-dozen steps away and said, "So long now, take care.''

When I left the apartment twenty minutes later there was a mustard yellow Toyota parked where his Jeep had been. The Jeep was chugging up the Merritt Parkway by then, heading for the New Hampshire woods. It was a long distance between West Seventy-fourth Street and the woodlands of New Hampshire. It was probably just as well that we were getting this relationship back to a professional basis. There was no point in feeling hurt and resentful. But I did.

Barbara Dannenberg's offices were on West Fifty-seventh, in a large building above an auto showroom. The corridors were pale and bleak, like a hospital without the personality. Bizarre names were lettered on the doors of our neighbors. I was particularly intrigued by the Mahjong League of America. I pictured squads of blue-haired matrons arriving in warm-up suits emblazoned with their team nicknames, mahjong boxes tucked under their arms, ready to square off for the league championship series.

My office was a small but friendly room high enough above the neighboring rooftops to allow the sun to brighten it most of the day. I had plenty to do. I had sorted through the inquiries of more than fifty interested writers who had been recommended to me either by editors, the grapevine, or the *Today* show plug. Some were veteran authors dissatisfied with their current representation, some were hopefuls looking for the same leap to success that Nathaniel Bumpers had made. I pulled the ten most interesting from the crop and drew the line there for the time being. Until I began to get the feel of things, I wanted to be sure I didn't spread myself too thin. My memories of Nanette Marx were still strong. I resolved not to take on any client whose telephone calls I would not return.

Under Barbara's tutelage and inspiration, I began to learn the rudiments of agentry. She would arrive at the office at nine o'clock with her energy level already humming. I would listen in awe as she worked the phones, cajoling, bargaining, threatening, flirting. She showed me how to set up a contract with the author's interests in mind and patiently taught me dozens of subtle tricks of the trade.

She also took me in hand for a fashion make-over. Barbara was in her middle thirties, a petite pretty woman who felt about style the way Adele Davis used to feel about vitamins. It wasn't only desirable, it was essential to life. Several times during our first weeks together I caught her looking at me with ill-concealed dismay.

"Sharon," she said to me one day, "if you're interested, I know a terrific hairdresser."

"You think I should do something different with my hair?" I was still wearing it pretty much as I had when I came East from Minneapolis, straight and full down my back, sometimes pulled up in a ponytail.

"I just think you ought to be doing *something* with it. You're so pretty, it just seems like a terrible waste of natural resources."

She meant it kindly. I decided to give it a try. The hairdresser, Lana, took pity on my nervous plea not to chop it too short, and I came out of the shop with a shoulder-length cut permed into a halo of frizz about my head. It took some time for me to recognize myself, but Barbara approved.

"Fabulous. I love it. Now you look like somebody. Now, I know some great boutiques. . . ."

During this period of my grooming, I was also hard at work. Editors who knew of the story of my discovery of Nathaniel Bumpers listened seriously to my recommendations, and I made good deals on several books, guided behind the scenes by the steadying hand of Barbara Dannenberg. But my main preoccupation was with the movie rights to *Man of Stone*.

As I had predicted to Nat, the field narrowed down quickly to three serious bidders. Paramount wanted it as a vehicle for Robert DeNiro. De Laurentiis was very interested and was dangling a package that included Louis Malle to direct and Christopher Walken to play the lead. The other contender was Tyler McGraw, the multithreat Oscar winner, who wanted it for himself to produce, direct, and star in. The figures being bandied about were staggering. The bidding had gone over four million. It made my palms sweat to even jot down all those zeroes on my telephone scratch pad. And there were still endless refinements and subtleties to be worked out before a decision could be reached.

One afternoon I was on the phone with a client when Barbara popped into my office. Her eyes were as round as silver dollars. "Hang up!" she mouthed, gesturing excitedly at me. I dispatched the client as quickly as I could.

"What is it? Russian tanks on Broadway?"

"He's here!"

"Who's here?"

"Tyler McGraw!"

"Where? Here in the office?"

"Yes! God, he's gorgeous. He does something funny to my knees. I almost needed a walker to get in here."

"Well, what does he want?"

"You, Sharon. He wants to see you!"

"Oh, my God. Do I have time to go home and change?"

"Don't worry, you look great. Are you ready for him?"

"Are you kidding? Okay, here goes. . . ."

I followed Barbara into the waiting room. There he was. Tyler McGraw. He was so handsome he seemed to suck the color from the air around him.

"Mr. McGraw," I said, "I'm sorry I kept you waiting."

He stood up, flashing that famous white-toothed, boy-next-door grin. He shook my hand.

"Not at all, Miss Clover. I know it was a presumption on my part just to drop in unannounced like this, but I'm in New York for the day and I was very anxious to meet you."

"Please, come into my office. Can I get you anything? Coffee? A drink?"

"No, no thanks. I know you're busy as hell here and I can't take up your time. What about dinner this evening, if you're not tied up? That would give us some time to talk. I'd like to have a chance to let you know how I feel about this book, how much the whole project means to me."

"Dinner . . . let me just check . . ." I made a show of going into my office and looking in my date book. I knew perfectly well that I had a date that evening with a beau of mine who was a commodities broker, and I knew just as well that he was going to have to make other plans for tonight.

"Yes," I agreed, smiling, "dinner would be fine."

"I had no idea you were so beautiful," Tyler McGraw said as he took my hand again in parting. "This evening is going to be a pleasure as well as business."

Barbara grinned at me from her doorway after Tyler McGraw had left. "Thank me," she said. "I made you presentable."

We dined at the Russian Tea Room. In a roomful of celebrities and beautiful people Tyler McGraw was the center of attention. He was tall, elegant, with jet-black hair that swept back from his forehead in smooth waves. His lips were full and the lower one tugged downward in almost a pout. His chin was broad, and deeply cleft. His smile was dazzling.

229

For myself, I was looking my best. I knew people were wondering who I was. When we left we were surrounded by autograph seekers and photographers. It was my first and last experience with paparazzi.

Tyler McGraw never took his eyes off me the whole evening. When he spoke about his admiration for *Man of Stone*, it was with deep sincerity. When I spoke, he listened to every word. Once or twice he touched my arm to emphasize a point, letting his hand linger a moment.

In the limousine I lay back against plush upholstery that smelled vaguely of spices and leather. Faces peered at the dark tinted glass as we pulled out into the traffic of Fifty-seventh Street. Tyler McGraw touched my arm.

"Shall I take you home? Or will you come have a nightcap with me? I'm using a friend's apartment while he's away."

I demurred, of course. And of course I accepted.

The friend had a nice home. It was a penthouse duplex on Sutton Place that looked like a movie set. It was decorated all in white: white sofa, white chairs, white carpeting, white on white paintings, white piano. Every moment I expected Fred Astaire to come dancing out in a top hat, white tie and tails.

But the real spectacle was from the balcony. The river was below us, beyond the luminous stream of traffic on the drive. The view extended for miles to the north and south. It seemed to take in all of eastern Manhattan. Out in the river tugs or barges moved at a slow pace through the black water and the mysterious islands of the river squatted darkly. Beyond was Queens, and dreary though it might be in the daytime, at night—

seen from across the river and reduced to a cipher of pale twinkling lights—it looked remote and lovely.

It was typical of all I had read and heard about Tyler McGraw that there should also be a full moon for the occasion.

He brought out a bottle of Veuve Cliquot and two chilled glasses to the balcony.

"You make the night so beautiful," he said. He eased the cork from the bottle with a soft sucking sound. "I didn't want to bring you inside just yet. I wanted to let you shine."

There must be a different critical standard for people of godlike beauty and for ordinary human beings. I wouldn't have listened to a line like that from anyone else. Coming from Tyler it made me melt. I sipped the cold champagne. The bubbles sped through my system into my pores.

When he filled my glass again he brought his face very close to mine, and looked into my eyes as he poured. I would have spilled doing that. Tyler didn't. He set down the bottle on the railing and kissed me on the throat. I arched my head backward to receive his kiss. . . .

I was Julie Christie, melting in wide-screen bliss under Tyler's legendary touch. I was Diane Keaton, gnawing at his ear as the camera came in for an extreme close-up. I felt his hand smoothly slide the zipper down the back of my dress. Would I do a nude scene? Would I not!

It was pure fantasy come to life. Not for nothing did Tyler McGraw have a reputation as Hollywood's greatest lover. Had he been able to translate this gift to the screen, he would have been known as Hollywood's greatest director.

The scene was brilliantly staged. The art direction—a fabulous penthouse, a terrace under the stars, a river lapping at the shore below, islands twinkling in the darkness beyond. A warm, perfumed night in early November, the last glorious surge of Indian summer. A gentle breeze. Music swelled on the soundtrack from digital quadrophonic speakers hidden somewhere among the shrubbery of the terrace, the lush romantic strains of Rachmaninoff's Third Symphony.

Tyler peeled my body bare. He caressed me, touching first my face—cheeks, nose, the curve of my eyebrows, the closed lids of my eyes, my lips. ''You're so beautiful,'' he murmured. He stood back so that he could only touch me with arms extended and his fingers trailed down barely skimming the flesh of my neck and arms. His eyes studied me with a look that would have brought jelly to the knees of Alice B. Toklas. He caressed me in erotically concentric circles, stroking the less erogenous zones until they responded with shivering ecstasy, then moving in to the classic parts. I was not to use my hands. When I tried to embrace him he shook his head and raised my arms above me. I was totally vulnerable, totally exposed. I began to tremble as he grazed the hard tips of my breasts. The million lights of the city were my audience, watching out of the darkness the greatest love scene ever filmed.

As Tyler worked his way with excruciating slowness to the core of my passion my whole body began to vibrate. I tried to keep still, but when he moved his caress to my ass, my hips began to move of their own accord to the rhythm of the low song that sprang from my throat. And when he brought two fingers in to the damp crease of my pussy, one from the back and one from the front, my legs lost their strength entirely and I sank against him, held up only by that penetrating saddle.

The night moved like cinema, through a series of dissolves to one erotic pinnacle and then another. I wasn't aware of his clothes coming off, only that he was more beautiful naked than clothed. He penetrated every part of me—my mouth and between my legs. Everything was ecstasy. I dissolved from climax to climax. I came at least a half-dozen times before he reached an orgasm, and then, incredibly, he was ready again. My juices kept flowing. He tapped in me the same seemingly bottomless capacity for sensual endurance that he possessed. In the end it was physical exhaustion, not sexual, that stopped him, and toward dawn we fell asleep. Fade to black.

Chapter 23

I didn't get to the office until eleven-thirty the next morning. Ralph, our secretary, handed me the mail and a stack of telephone messages. Barbara was on the phone, but a few minutes later barged into my office.

"Well?" she demanded. "Give!"

I looked up dreamily. "Hm?"

"As good as that?" She sank down into the guest chair. "Details, please."

"He's everything you've ever heard, ten times over."

"*Ten times*?"

"At least."

"Oh, Gawwwd!" She rolled her eyes ceilingward and simulated a faint. "I spent last night having dinner with a very boring gay editor, then went home and read myself to sleep with a manuscript on helpful hints for the homemaker."

"Well," I said, "there's no accounting for taste."

"Hah. So, are you going to see him again?"

"I don't know. Probably during the shooting."

Barbara sat up and looked at me sharply. "Hold it, Sharon. We're talking about two different things here. Tyler McGraw may be better in bed than Dino De Laurentiis, but that has nothing to do with Nat Bumpers. You can't let a night of multiple orgasms sway a decision like that."

"It's not that," I said defensively. "He's a brilliant film maker. *Henna* was a terrific movie."

"It wasn't bad," she admitted. "But that's not the point."

"What is the point?"

"Is he offering the best deal for your client? Will he make the best picture for your client? I'm not saying you're not a beautiful and sexy woman who any man would give a year's salary to go to bed with, but what happened last night was a tactic on Tyler McGraw's part. A hell of a good tactic, sure. He's welcome to try it on me. But it shouldn't affect your professional judgment one way or the other."

So I found myself driving north to New Hampshire. The leaves had turned and many of them had fallen, but a few trees still blazed bright yellow and red. Indian summer was gone and the air grew colder as I sped up the highway. I turned the heater on in the rented Ford Capri.

I checked into a motel on the outskirts of Peterborough, New Hampshire. It was four o'clock and I knew I wouldn't have the energy for the drive back to New

York that night. I asked the desk clerk if he knew where Potter's Road was.

"Potter's Road? Nope."

"Do you know Nathaniel Bumpers?"

"Ayuh."

"Isn't that where he lives? Potter's Road?"

"Well now, it might be. Might not be. Can't say as to that."

"Do you know where he lives?" I was doing my best to remain patient in the face of this maddening New Englandism. I've never had much use for that sort of local color.

"Let me see now. Natty Bumpers. Natty Bumpo, they used to call him. Like the fella in the Leatherstocking books, you know? *Last of the Mohicans,* now that was a fine book. Natty's writ himself a book now, I hear tell. Always was a strange one. Now, if you're interested in books, young lady, why . . ."

"I'm not interested in books! I'm interested in how to find Mr. Bumpers!"

"Natty Bumpers? Why sure. Through town, out past the Conklin plant, take the left by the Shell station. It's back in the woods about three miles. Not much of a road, what with snow comin'. If I was you . . ."

"Thank you very much." I picked up my key and hurried out to the car.

"Ought to read books," I heard him going on behind me. "It's television, that's what it is. Young folks don't read anymore." He was still talking as I passed beyond earshot. I doubt if my absence made any difference.

The road to Nat's house was truly awful. It was rutted and washed away on the inclines so that I had to drive way over on the side to keep from scraping off the bottom of the car. The harrowing drive revived the resentment of Nat that I thought I had buried. The remoteness of his cabin seemed in keeping with the remoteness he had shown me after our night of love. I gripped the wheel of my rented Ford like a drowning person clinging to a spar and negotiated a precarious passage through the woods until at last I came to Nat's little cabin.

It was getting dark. I pulled the rental car up next to the ancient Jeep. I got out and started to lock up, then realized that it was hardly necessary out here.

I stood there a moment, listening to the stillness. The windows of the cabin were lighted up and I could make out smoke coming from the chimney. Some sort of bird was singing. I am not good with birds. There was no other sound. It was eerie.

I knocked on the cabin door. After I had waited and there was no answer, I went around and peeked in the window. I couldn't see anybody inside. I tried the door. It was open. Feeling a little like Goldilocks, I went inside.

A few minutes later Nat appeared. He was naked, rubbing his head with a towel. When he saw me he became very embarrassed and covered himself quickly with the towel.

"I'm sorry," I said. "The door was open."

"No, that's okay. I was in the sauna and didn't hear you drive in. How are you?"

"Fine."

"I'll just get some clothes on."

I had left my briefcase with all the papers and figures in the car. I went out to get it. When I came back in he was dressed in jeans and a flannel shirt. He was scooping coffee from a can into a coffeepot. Now that he was dressed he was less ill at ease. But we were still formal with each other.

"I'm making coffee. Will you have some?"

"Thank you. I'm terribly sorry about barging in on you like this, but with no phone . . . You did get my letter?"

"Oh yes."

"The situation's pretty complicated. I thought we'd better go over it in person." I tried to smile. "And since you hate coming to New York so much, I thought I'd better bring the mountain to you."

I laid the stuff on the table. Nat brought me steaming black coffee in a tin cup. For the next several hours I sorted through the offers from the Big Three. Nat seemed to be paying attention, although he seldom asked any questions or expressed any opinion other than: "That sounds good."

I talked until I ran out of things to say. "That's about it. You'll want some time to think, you may want to talk to some other people. Why don't I leave all this with you, and you can call or drop me a line next week."

Nat shook his head with a wry grin. "I wouldn't know what to make of it. You decide."

"You want me to decide? But, Nat, there's an awful lot at stake here."

"A year ago I was just a guy living in the woods trying to write a book. All of a sudden I've got more money that I know what to do with. You've done all right for me so far. Whatever you decide is all right with me."

239

For some reason his complete trust annoyed me. Or perhaps it scared me. "All right," I said. "How about Tyler McGraw?"

Nat broke into a wide grin. "Tyler McGraw. That's something. Can you see me being played by Tyler McGraw?"

I was in a better position than most to judge, having played opposite them in the same scene, different productions. I suddenly saw that Tyler couldn't possibly get to the heart of the character that was Asa/Nathaniel. Perhaps Christopher Walken, under the skillful guidance of a great director like Louis Malle, might do it. It would mean curtains for my affair with Tyler. But it would make a better movie translation of *Man of Stone.*

It was completely up to me.

"Sure I can," I said. "Let's go with McGraw."

There was a surprise waiting for me when I went to leave. It was snowing outside. It was snowing hard. There were already two inches on the ground.

"How am I going to get out of here?"

"You won't make it in that car. I can run you into town in the Jeep, but you'd have to leave your car here."

"It's a rental. I can't just leave it."

"Then you'd better spend the night and see how things look in the morning."

So I stayed. Nat gave me the bed in his study-bedroom and he took the couch in the living room. It was the traditional male gesture in this sort of situation. Except that our situation wasn't exactly within the tradition. But we both seemed determined to act as though our night in New York had never happened.

In the morning it was still snowing. Three feet of powder were drifted against the door of the little cabin.

"You could be here for the winter," Nat observed as I gazed sullenly out at the white scenery.

"I'd better leave the car. Drive me to town and I'll try to rent another or get a bus or something."

"Too late for that. I won't be able to get out of here for a couple of days, at least."

"What? Jesus, how am I going to get back to New York?"

"Looks like you're not. Not today."

I sighed. "I'd better—oh shit, I can't even call, can I?"

"Nope."

"Jesus! What kind of a fucking place is this?" The redhead temper flared. I flung my coffee cup against the wall. Being tin it didn't break, but the coffee did splatter.

"I'm sorry," Nat said quietly. "I know this is a rotten inconvenience for you. Look, I'll snowshoe out and call your office for you."

"I'll snowshoe myself."

"Have you ever done it?"

"No," I admitted.

"With all this snow I doubt you'd even find the road. I'm afraid you're stuck here for a couple of days."

"Oh, that's great. That's really great."

Most anger comes from things not going the way we expect them to. A stubbed toe, a shopping bag caught in a door can change a person's whole mood.

241

What we control we tend to be at peace with. But I was in a situation now that was unexpectedly out of my control. It had upset my plans. And it had thrown me together, snowbound, with a man who upset me already. I was in a foul humor.

Nat was pulling on his heavy boots and a hooded parka. He took down a pair of snowshoes from the wall.

"Any special message for Barbara?"

"Yes, tell her next time to keep her advice to herself."

When Nat was gone, the stillness and total isolation spooked me. The snow was still falling. The trees at the far end of the clearing were just shadows through the veil of white. I could make out my rental car and the Jeep buried up to the fenders. A week ago it had been summer.

A week ago I had worn a bare-shouldered evening dress and had dined in the glittering bustle of the Russian Tea Room with Tyler McGraw and had felt that I was at the very heart of the civilized world. Now I stood in one of its bleakest outposts, wearing the oversized sweater of a reclusive writer who had awakened something vulnerable in me and then had run off to hide. And he had left me alone in the eerie silver silence, prey to God knew what terrors.

I looked about for a radio. I found one in the bookcase over the desk. It didn't work. I paced the cabin, alternately cursing Nat and praying for his return. After a while the snow stopped, but the day stayed bleak and sunless.

I tried to read. I picked up a copy of Turgenev's

nihilist classic, *Fathers and Sons*. But it was too quiet and I couldn't concentrate. I flipped through an issue of *Country Journal*. After awhile I put that aside.

Something happened to me. The peace filtered into my nervous system and the jangling stopped. It stopped suddenly, like a phone that has been ringing incessantly and then is not ringing anymore, but you aren't sure just when it stopped. I stood up and went to the door. The day had not changed. The air was still bleak and grey, the landscape still buried in white. But it was no longer hostile. It soothed me now. My muscles relaxed, my nerves quieted. My mind stopped racing and floated. And it came in touch with things that it had forgotten for a long time.

I had seen a jar of pencils and an empty yellow legal pad on Nat's desk. I got the pad and a pencil and came out to sit at the kitchen table. I put another log into the stove and poured myself a fresh cup of coffee. Then I started to write.

Chapter 24

I had filled half a dozen pages by the time Nat came back.

"I reached Barbara," he told me. "She said, and I quote, 'Well I certainly never advised her to get stuck out in the middle of nowhere in a blizzard without a telephone.'"

I laughed. "It's true, she didn't. Barbara would never get herself into a predicament like this."

"She said not to worry. She'll take care of things until you get back."

"I know she will." I watched him as he hung the snowshoes back on their nail. "Thanks for going, Nat. I really appreciate it."

He looked surprised. "Sure," he said.

"I've been a bitch. I apologize."

"That's okay. You had a right . . ."

"No, I didn't. I don't know what's the mat-

245

ter with me. I was up tight and I took it out on you."

"Too much city, maybe. It does that to me."

He made another pot of coffee and we sat and talked for a while. It was relaxed and comfortable, the way it had been in my apartment.

Nat saw that I had been writing.

"What is it?"

"It's nothing."

"A novel?"

I shrugged. "It's not really much of anything yet."

"Can I see it?"

"Oh no! Not on your life."

"Hey, I'm not a critic. I'd just like to see what you're writing."

"Maybe sometime," I demurred. "Not now. Anyway, you've got your own book to write. What kind of an agent would I be if I kept you sitting here talking and not doing your work?"

When he was back at his desk I picked up my pencil again. The fire crackled in the stove and the smell of wood smoke flavored the air with its faint sharpness. There was no traffic, no television, no telephone to ring. I poured myself a fresh cup of coffee and took up the thread of my story again. At first it was hard work and after a while it came more easily. What I was writing was the beginning of this book.

That night we went to bed in our separate and proper places. I fell asleep and after awhile I woke up with the feeling that something was different.

The room was light, with a pale silvery brightness that lit everything like an old daguerreotype. I got up and went to the window. The clouds had gone away and there was a full moon. The moonlight shone down on the snow, which gleamed and sparkled like powdered glass.

I went to the door of the living room. Nat was on the sofa. A cigarette ash glowed between his fingers.

"You're awake too? I think the moonlight woke me up."

"It's beautiful."

I came over and sat on the end of the sofa. "What I did today was the first writing I've tried to do in years. I haven't felt like it in a long time. I haven't slowed down enough to think that way. Today I remembered the feeling of wanting to write. But I'm not good at it yet. The muscles are atrophied. I don't want you to see it until it's better."

"That's okay. I don't want to push you. Whenever you're ready."

"I feel so vulnerable."

He chuckled softly. "I know. I feel that way too. All the time. I spent months trying to get up the courage to send you *Man of Stone*. And I didn't even know you. It's harder with someone you know."

I thought of him up here alone, writing the book that had now earned him a niche in American literature. It was strange to think that I hadn't known him then.

"Nat?"

"Yes?"

"Would you come to bed with me?"

He sat up on the sofa and took my hand. He stood up. The blanket fell away. He wasn't wearing anything. His body was pale and powerful in the unreal moonlight. He drew me up and put his arms around me. I was wearing one of his flannel shirts.

"Come on," he said. We went back to the bedroom.

We were snowed in for three days. During the daytime we wrote. In the evenings Nat would build a fire in the stone sauna, we would run down the path that he had cleared to bake in the heat, and then come out to roll naked in the snow.

I made a pretty good stew from the contents of his refrigerator, and it lasted us. After we had eaten at night we talked and he began to teach me chess. We made slow, delicious love in front of the fireplace, when we went to bed, and sometimes in the middle of the night.

On the third night I showed him what I had written. He seemed to like it. He was encouraging and had some good insights about ways I could improve it. He showed me his new book. It was extraordinary. It made me wonder why I even bothered, when I couldn't make my words sing as he did. But Nat made me see that our writing was different, that it was pointless to try to compare.

"Apples and oranges," he said.

"Champagne and soda pop."

"Arsenic and old lace."

"Penises and vaginas."

"Now you're talking."

On the next morning the town plow made it to the foot of Nat's hill. Then he was able to shovel us out. I felt almost betrayed when he came back to the house and told me it was clear. Again the awkwardness crept between us.

"I'll be in touch," I said. He had driven the Ford down the hill for me and now I was behind the wheel and he leaned on the open window.

"Good," he said.

"Nat, I've changed my mind about Tyler McGraw. I'm recommending the Louis Malle package."

"Whatever you say." He grinned. "I'm not the Tyler McGraw type, am I?"

"No." I stretched up my head and he bent down and kissed me. Then I drove south to New York.

Chapter 25

Mandy introduced me to Chapman Farrell. It was at a
party she gave that spring, six months after my stay at
Nat's cabin in Peterborough, New Hampshire.

"He's dissatisfied with his agent, kid," she told
me. "Play your cards right and you can have him
eating out of your pants. I've told him all about you."

"What have you told him?"

"Only the professional stuff. Anything else is up
to you."

Chapman Farrell. Winner of three National Book
Awards and two Pulitzer Prizes. He was already long
enshrined as a literary god when I took my American
Lit courses at Minnesota. Chapman Farrell was argua-
bly America's greatest living novelist, certainly one of
her most controversial. His private life—scratch that,
he had no private life—his personal life was more lurid
and sensational than the sort of fiction he disdained. He

once had been arrested for rape perpetrated upon the hostess at a glittering Park Avenue dinner party. After feverish behind-the-scenes negotiations, the charges somehow were dropped. He had taught a creative writing course at New Jersey's Rahway State Prison and had come under severe suspicion when two of his prize students had effected an escape, apparently in the trunk of Farrell's car. The fugitives had been recaptured and the affair had blown over.

Another arrest had followed a wild drunken night when he had tied up his wife naked in a bedsheet and dangled her out the window of their apartment, twelve floors above Sheridan Square. His wife had refused to press charges. She hadn't even left him, despite his many and much-publicized affairs with glamorous and celebrated women.

"You're the agent everybody's talking about," he said to me with a bantering stare. Farrell looked a bit older than I had expected. His was a heavy drinker's face with florid jowls, a red swollen nose, but eyes that were bright and intelligent beneath a cowl of bushy eyebrows. The wild curly hair that was so familiar from newspaper photos and David Levine caricatures in *The New York Review of Books* was heavily laced with grey.

"You're certainly the writer everyone's talking about," I answered him.

"You by any chance referring to my recent scrape with the law?"

His latest escapade had involved four hundred pounds of Colombian gold that had been discovered in the boathouse on his Sag Harbor estate. Farrell's lawyers had been able to show that he hadn't set foot on Long Island in ten months and knew nothing of the

cache of contraband. Two Colombians and a Nicara-
guan student who had once worked for Farrell were
subsequently indicted in absentia by a grand jury, but
they hadn't been apprehended. They were generally
assumed to have left the country.

"Not at all, Mr. Farrell. I was referring to your
literary accomplishments. Your new book is brilliant."

"Well, thank you," he said. His eyes sparkled
attractively when he smiled, and I began to see where
his reputation as a lover came from. "I like an agent
who appreciates literature, especially when she's young,
redheaded and beautiful as a morning in Killarney. My
agent doesn't know his ass from a bodice buster and
he's middle-aged, bald, and has a face like a trash can
lid besides." He patted my hand. "Perhaps we can do
something together."

From the look in his eye, from the tone of his
voice, from everything I knew about Chapman Farrell,
I was sure that he was talking about something more
than the standard agent/author contract.

"Perhaps we can," I replied.

I had already had a lot to drink when we left
Mandy's party. Farrell had easily consumed twice as
much as I had, but it had no discernible effect on him
except perhaps to make him sound more Irish. We
stopped off for a few more in the Lion's Head. I hadn't
been there in a long time. It brought back vivid memories of my early days in New York. I looked around
half-expecting to see Liam, though I knew he was in
Hollywood now.

"So you wanted to be a writer, did you? And what
made you stop, then?"

253

"It was a biological problem. I needed to eat."

"You never published anything?"

I grimaced. "A Gothic novel."

"A Gothic novel?" He looked astounded. "Why on earth would you do that?"

"I was broke," I said defensively. "Anyway, I thought it would be a good experience for me to write *something* and see it published. Good practice."

Farrell shook his great shaggy head in disagreement. "It's a mistake. Writing's not that sort of thing. You can't slop it out like that, you use it up. It's not like the dance, or piano, where you keep at the top only by constant repetition. It's not like being an athlete, where you take a hundred swings in batting practice, hit a hundred serves, whack a hundred balls off the practice tee. No, writing's a precious, limited quantity. We've each got so much and there's no knowin' how much it is. Each bit you use, there's that much less left in the reservoir. Don't dribble it away on crap, darlin'. It won't be there when you need it."

Later we left the Lion's Head and went to Farrell's apartment. It was a spacious old Greenwich Village flat with high windows and ceilings, many hallways and rooms. Farrell went through turning on lights.

"A drink," he boomed. "That's what we need! That's what's wrong with this city—nothin' to drink! Aha! Whiskey. Pride o' the Scotsman's art. Miracle in a bottle. Lovely people, the Scottish. Nancy! Where are ye, girl? Come drink with us. We've got company."

A sleepy blonde woman of about thirty-eight appeared. She was wearing a large tee shirt that had NUKE THE NARCS lettered on it. She was rubbing her eyes.

"There she is! Nancy, my pet, meet Sharon Clover. Sharon is a great agent. Wouldn't know it to look at her, would you? Nancy is my wife. Wouldn't know it to look at me, would you? A woman of infinite patience, faithful and true. God knows why she puts up with me. A drink, Nance? Whiskey?"

She gave a sleepy shrug of a smile and put her hand out to me. "Pleased to meet you, Sharon." She took the drink Farrell offered her. He fixed a tall Scotch for himself, and one for me. It was the last thing I needed, but I took it, under the spell of the legendary hard-drinking author.

I had been surprised to find Farrell's wife at home. But from what I knew of Farrell, nothing could surprise me very much. I found myself looking at her with peculiar fascination, picturing her buxom figure trussed in a bedsheet and suspended nude from the window.

"Puts up with a lot from me," Farrell declared, perhaps guessing my thoughts. "But we have some times together too, don't we darlin'? Oh, I keep her happy."

"It's his cock," she told me smilingly. "His great cock. Has he shown it to you yet?"

"No," I said. "Not yet."

Nancy chuckled. "He will. He always does."

"Aye, and why not? 'Tis a man's proudest possession. That's what separates him from woman. Women don't have 'em, you see. Did 'e know that, little Sharon? Here, look—I'll show you."

He held up his wife's nightshirt, exposing a full blonde bush. "You see that? Nothin' there! Well, not quite nothing. 'Tis a quim they've got. Oh, delectable little things!" With two fingers he parted the fur, revealing the pink lips hidden there. "A lot to be thankful for," he murmured, "a lot to be thankful for."

Nancy sipped her drink and stood with a blurry smile on her face.

"Turn around, my dear. Let's show her all. No secrets. There's more to see," he confided to me. Nancy turned her back and Farrell lifted the tee shirt to show me her ass. "Where in all literature is there an image as sublime as a lady's bottom?" He gave it a smack. The cheeks quivered.

"All right then. Off to bed now, darlin'. I've some business to discuss with little Sharon."

The smile never left her pretty dumpling face. "All right," she agreed. She shook my hand again. "If it gets too late, dear, you're welcome to sleep over on the couch."

I did feel bad, but the liquor in my veins was sufficient insulation against the cold winds of conscience. But later, when we had undressed and Farrell had introduced me to the rampant phallus that was the source and mainstay of his masculine pride, when he had introduced it into me and was rutting gaily away on top of me singing "What Shall We Do With the Drunken Sailor," I saw her lurking in the darkened hallway, watching us. I couldn't tell whether or not she was still smiling.

Chapter 26

It wasn't, I think, on the basis of that night that I acquired Chapman Farrell as a client. Farrell was no pussy-drunk adolescent. When he hired me, it was based on his educated belief that I would do the job for him professionally.

And I did. Shortly after that I negotiated a deal for his next book that made the talk of *Publishers Weekly*. I was inundated with direct and circuitous inquiries from authors, famous authors, who wanted to know if I could perform some similar feat for them.

What room my business schedule left for a social life was constantly full. I was dating a young congressman who was running for the United States Senate, a broadway composer and a Spanish Grand Prix racing driver.

Mandy had been in Europe and China on tour for a number of months. When she came back that fall, I broke a date with the politician and had Mandy over for dinner.

When I checked the mail as I was coming home that evening, there was a postcard from Nat. It was a home-made postcard on a photograph he had taken of the cabin. The sun was streaming down in stripes through the summer woods and the meadow was dotted with flowers. It read:

Having a wonderful time. Wish you were too.

Over dinner Mandy told me about her trip. She was ecstatic about China, and I listened enviously. But now and then my mind wandered to Nat and his post card.

"Is something bothering you, kid? You don't look as happy as a superstar agent ought to look."

"Me? No, I'm great."

"Sure, I know that. But are you fine?"

I laughed. "Mind your own business and put this silver chest away for me, will you?"

"Where does it go?"

"Up in that closet. And if it disappears next time I'm away for a weekend, I'll know where to send the law."

"Big deal. I know how to handle cops."

I finished up the dishes and made coffee. When I came out Mandy was sitting on the sofa. She had a yellow legal pad in her hands and was reading.

"This is great, Sharon," she said seriously, look-ing up at me with her brown eyes. "When did you write this?"

"Oh, a while ago. When I was up at Nat Bumpers'

place that time and it snowed." I poured the coffee and handed her a cup.

"Why don't you stick with it? Try to finish it."

I shrugged. "I've tried a couple of times. I can't seem to get into it."

Mandy looked at me for a long time until I blushed under her gaze and looked away.

"I don't understand you sometimes, Sharon. If I could write like this. . . ."

"You don't have to write. You're a great dancer."

"Yes. And if I didn't dance, I'd die. I'd wither up."

After Mandy left that night I read again what I had written on that yellow pad. I started to cry. I sat in my windowseat and tilted up my head and looked at my little sliver of sky. I knew that it was a clear night, but I couldn't see any stars. I was twenty-six years old and I could remember only three days in the last five years when I had really been happy.

The road was as rutted and impossible as I remembered it. I edged way over to the side and negotiated the steep rise. Branches scraped against the side of the car, showering yellow leaves in through the open window.

When I reached the clearing I saw that the skeleton of a new room was attached to the cabin. Nat was sitting up on one of the beams, wearing sneakers and a pair of cutoff jeans. He was hammering a nail. I sat on the hood of the car and watched him for a while before he noticed that I was there.

"Hello," he smiled. "What are you doing here?"

"I can't tell. Does that mean you're glad to see me or you're not glad to see me?"

He swung down off the building and came over to me. He was sweating and unshaven, he looked beautiful. He kissed me.

"Then you *are* glad to see me?"

"That's not a screwdriver in my pocket."

I glanced down. "Don't look now," I said, "but it ain't altogether in your pocket."

"By golly. Maybe I did cut these things too short."

"What are you building?"

He stood back and looked over at the rough pine armature. "That's your study," he said. "Only you got here a little earlier than I figured."

"My study?"

"We'll each need a place to write."

I slipped my hand into his. "Did you really know I'd come?"

"No," he said. "You surprised me there."

"Well, then. . . ."

"I figured I'd have to come and get you."

I moved away from him toward the house, then I looked back over my shoulder and smiled. "Come and get me."